ChangelingPress.com

Savage/Against The Wall Duet

Harley Wylde

Savage/Against The Wall Duet
Harley Wylde

ISBN: 978-1-60521-828-1

Publisher:
Changeling Press LLC
315 N. Centre St.
Martinsburg, WV 25404
ChangelingPress.com

Printed in the U.S.A.

Editor: Crystal Esau
Cover Artist: Bryan Keller

The individual stories in this anthology have been previously released in E-Book format.

Table of Contents

Savage (Devil's Fury MC 10) 4
    Prologue 5
    Chapter One...9
    Chapter Two 19
    Chapter Three...27
    Chapter Four...41
    Chapter Five 59
    Chapter Six..71
    Chapter Seven 82
    Chapter Eight..99
    Chapter Nine 116
    Chapter Ten 129
    Chapter Eleven..139
    Chapter Twelve 153
    Epilogue 164
Against the Wall (A Bad Boy Romance) 169
    Chapter One...170
    Chapter Two 180
    Chapter Three...190
    Chapter Four...198
    Chapter Five 204
    Chapter Six..210
    Chapter Seven 218
Harley Wylde...228
Changeling Press E-Books 229

Savage (Devil's Fury MC 10)
Harley Wylde

Mariah -- I knew my dad, a Dixie Reaper, wouldn't understand why I wanted to date a cop. I'd planned to elope with Ty, until it all went so very wrong. My dad caught me, tossed me in the car, and drove me to the Devil's Fury. I didn't know he'd already promised me to Savage, the Devil's Fury MC Treasurer. A man who set butterflies loose in my stomach at first sight. The man might have claimed me as his, but he runs every time we're in the same room. Whatever it is, he needs to let me go or make me his -- in all ways.

I never expected the surprise left at the gates and the way it would make my heart break, or that my ex would be a lunatic. I should have known life would throw me a curveball. Or two. Nothing is ever easy.

Savage -- Claiming a woman sight unseen didn't seem like such a bad thing. The fact she's two decades younger than me might have given me pause at one point, but not anymore. Then she arrives, spitting and hissing like an angry kitten. I try to do the right thing and give her time. Clearly that was the wrong thing to do.

The dirty cop who preys on women and children will be taught a lesson he won't soon forget. Should have known the daughter of a Dixie Reaper wouldn't shy away from getting her hands dirty and wouldn't need saving. Not sure how I got so lucky but I'm holding on tight to Mariah. She's the best thing to ever happen to me.

Prologue

Mariah
Three Months Earlier

My heart slammed against my ribs as I slipped out of the house and hurried to my car. So far, no one had questioned me being gone more than usual. Each time I pulled away from the compound, I breathed a sigh of relief at not getting caught. I knew my dad would have a fit if he knew who I'd been dating. He wouldn't give Ty a chance. He'd take one look at the badge attached to his shirt and that would be the end of it.

I drove through town and kept going. We'd decided it would be safer to meet in the next town over. My dad's club went there on occasion, but it wouldn't be as likely I'd run into anyone I knew. I saw Ty's SUV parked outside the diner and butterflies erupted in my stomach as I pulled in next to him. I checked my hair and lipstick before getting out and heading inside.

Ty waved at me from a table in the back and I hurried over. Smiling broadly, I slipped into the seat across from him. We'd been dating a few months, and I just knew he was *the one*. He'd been so sweet, so attentive. We hadn't gone as far as I'd have liked, but we'd kissed, and he'd touched me a few times. Last time I'd even given him a blow job.

"There's my beautiful girl," he said, giving me a wink. "Any trouble getting away?"

I shook my head. "I don't think they suspect anything."

"Good. I already ordered for us." He leaned across the table and lowered his voice. "I have something special planned when we're done."

If I'd thought I had butterflies earlier, I must have had pterodactyls swooping through my stomach now. Something special? I wondered where we'd be going, or what he had in mind.

Our food arrived and I gave the salad a baleful glance, but at least I had some baked chicken and carrots to go with it. I knew he hadn't meant anything insulting by ordering me rabbit food, and I'd choke it down just for him, but I'd have much preferred a burger and fries.

"How was work?" I asked, hoping he wouldn't notice my lack of enthusiasm over my meal.

"Good. Stopped a burglary over on Pine Road, but otherwise I just dealt with routine traffic stops."

I nodded. "I'm glad you stayed safe. I know your job can be dangerous."

He grinned. "Can't take me down easily. Besides, you give me a reason to keep breathing."

My cheeks warmed and I ducked my head. I felt all fluttery inside when he said stuff like that. I'd never dated anyone like him before. I knew he was quite a bit older than me, but it didn't matter. Not to me. Age was just a number, after all. At least, that's how it had always seemed. I knew my dad was roughly two decades older than my mom.

We finished our meal, and he left enough money on the table to cover everything plus tip, then he placed his hand at my lower back and guided me outside. I always loved when he did that. It made me feel like a princess or something. We stopped beside his SUV, and he popped the locks before helping me inside.

"I'll bring you back to your car in a bit. No sense taking two vehicles," he said.

I knew he was right, but I couldn't help but

worry someone would recognize my car. If anyone
from the Dixie Reapers happened by, they'd wonder
where I was, and more importantly, why I'd strayed so
far from home.

Ty pulled away from the diner and reached over
to hold my hand. His thumb caressed my skin and I
sighed in contentment. I loved when he did things like
that. He pulled over at a park and I waited while he
came around to my door. I'd learned the hard way not
to get out on my own. He helped me down and led me
down the pathway. A small lake glistened in the
sunlight as we stepped through the trees.

"Oh, Ty. It's beautiful."

"Not as beautiful as you." He dropped to his
knee and smiled up at me. "I know this is sudden, and
you're still young, but I love you, Mariah. Will you
please be my wife? Make me the happiest man ever?"

Tears misted my eyes, and my throat grew tight.
"Yes. Yes, Ty. I'll marry you."

He slid a ring onto my finger. The band was thin
and the diamond tiny, but I didn't care. It was perfect.
I'd have to hide it from my family. For now, anyway.
They'd have to meet him sooner or later.

He stood and wrapped his arms around me,
kissing me long and deep. I didn't know when we'd
get married, or where, but I didn't care. As long as I
was Ty's at the end of the day, nothing else mattered. I
wanted so badly to call my sister and tell her the news,
but if I did, she'd tell Demon and then he'd call my
dad. I couldn't risk it. For now, I'd keep the
engagement to myself.

"I'll make the arrangements in a few months," Ty
said. "Until then, we'll meet when we can. You've
made me so happy, Mariah."

"I'm happy too," I murmured, kissing him again.

"So happy."

It never occurred to me my happily-ever-after would fall to pieces. But I should have known better. If there was anything my dad wouldn't stand for, it was me getting married to a cop.

Chapter One

Mariah

My jaw ached from grinding my teeth. I stared out the window, refusing to even look at my dad. I couldn't believe he'd hauled me away from Tyson. Another few minutes, and we'd have been gone. I wondered who'd told. Could have been the Prospect at the gate, or any of my dad's spies around town. I should have waited until dark. Even though I'd begged Ty to wait, he hadn't listened.

"Can't ignore me forever," my dad said.

Want to bet?

We crossed the Alabama state line and entered Florida. He hadn't said exactly where we were going. Devil's Boneyard? They weren't far from our current location. I wanted to ask. Pressing my lips together, I forced myself to remain silent.

"Fine. Pout like a damn kid, Mariah, but it's not going to change anything. Settle in. We still have a bit of a drive."

I looked over at him. What the hell did that mean? The Devil's Boneyard was only another hour, if that. So where were we going? When he took the ramp to head north into Georgia, my stomach knotted. Oh, shit.

"We're going to see Farrah?" I asked before I could stop myself.

"Nope, but same location."

Shit. If we weren't going to see Farrah, then who? Did my dad want my brother-in-law, Demon, to scare the hell out of me? Because it wouldn't be hard. Just being in his presence was enough to make me pee myself. I knew he doted on my sister, but it didn't change his scare factor. I'd heard the stories of what he'd done when people crossed him or the Devil's Fury.

I tried not to fidget as the truck ate up the miles. My nerves were shot by the time we arrived. Expecting my dad to stop at Farrah's or even the clubhouse, I couldn't hold back my gasp as he kept going. Bile rose in my throat, and I scanned the area, not having a damn clue whose house we'd be visiting. The fact he'd packed my clothes and a box of my books didn't bode well for this being a quick stop.

Since my dad had taken my phone, I couldn't even text Ty to let him know my current location. I knew he'd have come for me. We may not have made our flight today, but we could have gotten another one.

We came to a stop outside a sprawling home. It might have only been one-story, but I could tell it was far from small inside. I got out and stood by the truck, not knowing what to expect. The front door opened and when I saw the large man who strolled out to meet us, my stomach flipped.

"You made good time," Savage said, holding his hand out to my dad.

"Needed to get her out of there immediately. Caught her trying to run off with the cop." My dad glared at me. "Nothing to say, Mariah?"

"Why am I here?" I asked.

Savage's eyebrows rose and he rocked back on his feet. "Damn. I'm guessing this is a conversation we should have inside. Y'all come in. Need me to get anything from the truck?"

"I threw a box of her books in the back seat, and she has a bag of clothes. I can send the rest in a few days." My dad started walking to the house. "Getting old's a bitch. I'm using your bathroom."

Savage snickered.

My dad tossed a phone at him. "That's hers. She can have it back, but I'm not giving it to her. She may call that shithead cop."

Savage caught the phone, looked at it a moment, then handed it to me. "No calls or texts until we talk. Don't make me regret letting you have that back."

He opened the back door of the truck and hauled my stuff out like it didn't weigh anything. I had no choice but to follow him into the house. He set my things down inside the door and motioned for me to have a seat in the living room. Gray slate floors stretched in every direction, and the light gray walls added to the drab color scheme.

I sank onto a black leather sofa and eyed the unusual coffee table. It had to be custom-made. The base looked like a large cut tree trunk. Etched into the top were the colors for the Devil's Fury, and a piece of glass set over the top, cut to match the edges. I hadn't ever seen anything like it. The wood had been distressed or stained to a dark charcoal.

To my left, a flat screen TV hung from the wall. It had to be at least sixty inches or more. Across from the couch and table were two chairs, and a smaller table set between the two. An ottoman sat catty-corner to one of them, and I figured it must be where Savage usually sat. The chair looked more worn than the other one.

My dad entered the room, his arms folded, and he glared at me. I narrowed my eyes right back and waited to see why he'd brought me here.

"What did you mean you caught her trying to leave with the cop?" Savage asked, sinking into one of two leather chairs, the one I'd thought would be his. He sprawled, reminding me of a big jungle cat.

"Ty and I are getting married," I said.

Savage tensed. "That right?"

"I didn't tell her," Dad said. "I should have, but I was biding my time."

Savage arched an eyebrow. "That worked out well, didn't it?"

The look they shared told me something was up. Why had my dad brought me here? What had he kept from me?

"Tell me what?" I asked.

"Casper VanHorne arranged for Savage to claim you as his old lady. You're already promised to him, Mariah, so you can't marry the damn cop."

I shot to my feet. "What? Are you serious right now?"

My heart raced. What had Casper done? Or my father, for that matter. How could they have done this? I'd always thought I'd have a say in who I ended up with. I'd known my dad would never accept Tyson, but I'd thought he'd come to tolerate him eventually. But this?

"Back up a minute," Savage said. "Exactly how were you going to get married? You're only seventeen."

"Right. You *claimed* a teenager. Sick bastard," I muttered.

My dad growled and advanced on me. I sat quickly, knowing I'd gone too far. He hunkered down in front of me, looking all kinds of pissed off. At least I knew he wouldn't hit me. He'd never hurt any of us, no matter how loud he yelled. Although, it hadn't stopped him from taking away our electronics, forbidding us from leaving the house, or coming up with unusual punishments we always hated.

"You think Savage claiming you is any different from that fucking cop saying he would marry you?

Because Savage is right, Mariah. I saw your forged documents. The cop had to get them for you. But I don't think you thought everything through," Dad said.

I felt my cheeks burn as I sank farther into the cushions, wishing I could disappear. I shouldn't have asked Ty for those. If he'd kept them, my dad wouldn't have found them. For that matter, maybe I could have slipped away a little later. If he hadn't known what we planned, I might still be in Alabama.

"Forged? What the hell did she have?" Savage asked.

"Birth certificate and license claiming she's nineteen," Dad said before looking at me again. "Did it not occur to you that you'd eventually have to come home? It's where that dipshit works, and the entire fucking town knows you're not even eighteen yet."

Savage stood, his hands fisted at his sides. "What the fuck?"

He shared a look with my dad, and I knew whatever they were thinking wouldn't be good. But they were wrong! Ty loved me! We'd been seeing each other in secret for half a year. My cheeks warmed when I remembered all our stolen moments. He hadn't taken my virginity, saying he wanted to save it for our wedding night, but we'd done other things.

"Mariah, listen good, you hear me?" Dad tapped my knee to make sure he had my attention. "He didn't plan on returning with you. There's no damn way possible he'd have pulled it off. Did you see the plane tickets with your own eyes? Both for your trip there and the return tickets?"

I hesitated. No, I hadn't. He'd told me we were going to Las Vegas to get married, and I'd trusted him. He hadn't had a reason to lie, right?

"How many are missing?" Savage asked softly.

My dad focused on him. "Three that I'm aware of. None of ours until now."

Missing? My brow furrowed. I didn't know what was going on. What was missing and what did it have to do with me?

"Wait. What are you talking about?" I asked.

Savage sighed and came closer, kneeling on my other side. He reached for my hand, and I let him take it. "Little girl, your daddy just saved you from being sold. That cop you're so hung up on? He wasn't going to marry you. There's no way possible he could have managed it. The moment you returned home, your dad would have raised hell, and the marriage would have been annulled. Not to mention, the cop would be facing a statutory rape charge if he'd touched you, assuming he's older than nineteen, and taking a minor across state lines without the parents' permission is a federal offense."

I digested his words and saw the sincerity in his eyes. He believed every word he'd just said, and a glance at my dad proved he felt the same way. Sold? They really thought Ty had planned to get me away from home and then sell me? No. Every touch, every kiss had told me how much he wanted me. There was no way he'd do something like that. Plus, he was a police officer! If I could trust anyone, it would be Tyson.

"You're wrong. Ty loves me." I tilted my chin up. "We've been dating for months."

Oops. Wrong thing to say. If my dad were a cartoon character, steam would be pouring from his ears right now.

"He's been grooming you for months!" My dad started pacing. "Jesus, Mariah. For someone so smart, you're being a dumbass. Think about Rin. Her own brother turned her into a whore. You really think your precious cop isn't capable of the same thing?"

Rin's brother had been a pimp before he'd done that to her. Of course, I didn't think Ty was anything like that monster!

"She doesn't know what you've been working on," Savage said. "I think you should tell her."

My dad sighed and stared at the ceiling a moment before nodding his head. "All right. Chief Daniels went to visit his daughter at the Reckless Kings. He mentioned to Hawk and Beast a few problems he'd been having around town. Our town. Teen girls between the ages of fifteen and seventeen are going missing. Three so far, but I have a feeling you were about to be number four. They've been spaced about four to six months so as not to draw attention."

Sounded more like runaways to me. Or maybe their dads had been just as overbearing as mine. Why didn't anyone consider they simply wanted to have a life of their own? Not to mention, four to six months? That was a pretty big gap if someone was stealing girls and selling them.

"Then why does he think they're related?" I asked.

"Because each one was seeing someone in secret, a guy they said loved them. Each confided in a friend they were going to run away with this guy. After finding you and that damn cop were ready to run off today, I think your precious Ty is the one luring them away. Who the hell wouldn't trust a baby-faced cop like him? He's supposed to be the good guy," Dad said.

I wanted to argue, to defend Ty, but... All those girls had been secretly dating someone, just like me.

And Ty was the one who'd said we needed to keep things quiet, claimed my family would never understand. I'd fallen for every word out of his mouth.

"You really think he was going to sell me?" I asked, feeling betrayed, and incredibly stupid. Three girls? Had Ty really dated them, like he'd been doing with me? Had he promised them a happily-ever-after, and they'd been just as gullible as me? Or had he been working with someone else?

My dad nodded. "I do. I'm going to take your forged documents to the chief and let him know about Tyson Clarke. He'll have to investigate, but I'm not taking any chances. You're going to stay here with Savage, where you belong."

I looked over at the man who'd claimed me without my knowledge. I couldn't tell his age, but I knew he had to be closer to my dad's age than mine. Or maybe somewhere between the two of us. Being with an older man didn't bother me. Officer Clarke had been in his mid-twenties. Now that I knew he'd been trying to get me away from the safety of my family, I had to wonder why I didn't question his attention. Grown men didn't typically date teen girls. I might have been surrounded by couples who were anywhere from eight years to a few decades apart in age, but none of them had been minors. Well, not quite. Technically Torch had claimed Isabella when she'd been seventeen, but he hadn't touched her until she'd become a legal adult.

"Do I have a property cut?" I asked.

A slight smile curved Savage's lips. "Of course, baby girl. I have the spare room set up for you. It's hanging in your closet."

I'd already let one man run over me, and I wasn't about to make the same mistake. Letting Tyson have complete control over our relationship had nearly gotten me kidnapped. I knew Savage wouldn't do anything of the sort, but I didn't want him to think I was a pushover either.

I folded my arms. Once again, people were planning my life and I was supposed to sit on the sidelines and follow instructions. I didn't like it and wondered just how far I could push him. What would it take to make him crack?

Clearly, I had no choice in being his. I knew how shit worked with the clubs, and my dad had as good as sold me to Savage. Walking away wasn't an option. It wasn't that I didn't find him attractive. Any woman with eyes would admire him. Still, it didn't mean I had to be a doormat. Could I fluster the big guy? "And if I don't want a spare room?"

He stood abruptly and backed up a step, shaking his head. "Nope. Not going there until you're older. Until you're a legal adult, you're staying in the guest room."

Oh, this was good. No, it was excellent. I loved the dread flashing in his eyes and nearly smiled. I pulled out my phone and searched the Internet for age of consent in the state of Georgia. When I found the answer, I showed it to him. "Says right here age of consent in this state is sixteen."

Savage looked to my dad with a panicked expression. "Help me out here, Venom."

My dad lifted his hands and backed all the way up to the doorway. "Not going there. She's now your problem. But I've got to say, if the two of you do have sex, I don't want to hear about it. Ever. Not even ten years from now when she's nearly thirty. Far as I'm concerned, she'll be a virgin forever and any grandbabies you give me will be from an immaculate conception."

I rolled my eyes and ignored my dad. For such a badass, he became extremely squeamish when it came to his girls and certain topics. If I weren't the subject of today's trip down the road of denial, I'd have found it hysterical.

Looked like I'd have to prove to Savage I could handle him, and the Devil's Fury. Heaven help me. I wasn't sure I was up for the task, but I'd damn sure try.

Chapter Two

Savage

I couldn't believe the little spitfire had wanted to move her things into my room. I didn't know when she turned eighteen. Probably should have asked. While a few months didn't make much difference, I knew the club would feel better if I waited. Hell, so would I. Venom hadn't stayed long afterward. Instead of taking another room in the house, he'd opted to stay elsewhere. Couldn't blame him. Mariah kept glaring at him, and while I knew she was far better off here than anywhere near Officer Clarke, it would take her some time to get over it.

I wondered if anyone had even considered it could be a cop luring those young women from their homes. He had the perfect set-up. If anyone reported a girl missing, he'd be at the police station to hear about it. And when Chief Daniels decided to ramp up his investigation, he'd have had the inside scoop. It would have permitted him to stay one step ahead. Until he fucked up and picked Mariah.

I paused outside her door, lifting my hand only to let it drop again. As much as I wanted to check on her, she probably needed some space. Poor thing had woken up this morning planning to marry a guy she'd thought loved her, only to be dropped here and told she belonged to a stranger. I couldn't imagine how she felt right now.

I kept moving and went to my bedroom, shutting the door. Flopping back on my bed, I stared up at the ceiling and wondered what the hell I would do with Mariah. When I'd agreed to claim her, I'd thought someone would explain everything to her. Prepare her. Nope. Those fuckers had left her in the dark. I didn't want to be the bad guy in her eyes. I'd planned to take the time between now and her birthday to get to know her and let her become comfortable being around me. Now I didn't know what the fuck to do.

Ever since I'd agreed to claim her, and had a property cut made, I hadn't touched another woman. It hadn't mattered to me she was young and wouldn't be in my bed. Far as I was concerned, I was off the market from that moment onward. My brothers had given me shit over it, except those who already had women. They'd understood. And I think Farrah had respected me a little more for my loyalty to her sister. Why hadn't Farrah ever mentioned anything to her? At first, I hadn't realized Demon had told her anything, but from a few comments Farrah had made, I knew she was aware I'd claimed her younger sister. Her old man had to have told her. Unless someone else told their old lady and it spread through the club as the women gossiped.

The fact Mariah's entire family, and the Dixie Reapers, kept it from her made me both angry on her behalf, and apprehensive over how things would progress between us. What if she never accepted my claim? It was possible she'd resent me. Despite her flirty comment earlier, I didn't think for a minute she actually wanted to share my bed. She *had* been flirting, hadn't she? I hadn't spent much time with women in so long I was severely out of practice. With the club whores, talking wasn't necessary. You snapped your fingers, and they did what you wanted.

The more I thought about it, I realized she couldn't have been serious about sharing my bed. At least, not right now. She'd more than likely been trying to throw me off my game and get even with Venom.

It made me wonder exactly how experienced she

was when it came to men. How far had Officer Clarke gone? Virgins usually held a higher value, except in rare cases. Had he been grooming her for a special sort of client? Training her to please her new master? The thought sickened me. If I ever got my hands on that asshole, I'd rip his spine out.

My phone rang and I pulled it from my pocket, seeing Demon's name on the screen.

"Hello."

He growled, "Why the hell is Venom setting up in my guest room right now?"

I held back my laughter -- barely. I should have known he'd go there. After all, his eldest daughter lived with Demon. "Mariah isn't too pleased to be here. I think he's giving her some space. Why? Isn't Farrah happy to see her dad?"

"You know damn well she is, but I can't very well fuck my woman with her dad right down the hall. Thanks a lot, fucker."

"Not my doing. He dropped Mariah here without preparing her at all. She had no clue I'd claimed her. It's a big clusterfuck if you ask me. I have no damn idea what to do right now. Do I leave her alone? Make her spend time with me?"

Demon snorted. "You're asking the wrong person."

"I thought maybe you could ask your woman. They're sisters after all."

"You want to ask Farrah how to get into her baby sister's pants?" Demon asked.

I winced. "Not exactly. I already told Mariah I wouldn't touch her until she's eighteen. I'm just not sure if I need to try and get to know her better, or back off a bit. She's had a shock, Demon."

"Yeah. Sounds like Venom fucked up this time. I

already heard why he dropped her off today. It apparently didn't occur to him to say something to her sooner. Maybe it would have kept her from trying to run off with the guy. Or it could have made her run sooner. We'll never know."

The thought of my woman running from me made my gut clench. I could have had my pick of any woman I'd taken to my bed over the years. And even some I hadn't. Not once had I ever been tempted to keep one. Well, not since I was still a punk-ass teen. I hadn't been much older than Mariah when I'd fallen fast and hard for a girl in town. I wished I'd seen the signs. Paid closer attention. I'd thought she loved me as much as I'd loved her. Until the day I went to her house, knocked on the door, and had been greeted by her grieving parents. She'd taken her life. The note she'd left had said she'd felt trapped in her relationship with me.

I didn't want to put another woman in that position ever again. Not Mariah. Not anyone. I'd had plenty of women ease the ache of loneliness one night at a time, but I'd never once tried to have more than that with them. Not since Ellie.

I'd thought things would be different with Mariah. She'd grown up with the Dixie Reapers and knew how club life worked. Had I been wrong? Maybe it hadn't been that Ellie didn't want a life in the Devil's Fury. I'd always assumed that's what she'd meant. She hadn't wanted to be a biker's old lady, and she hadn't known how to tell me. Now I had to wonder, had she just not wanted to be with *me*? If that was the case, what if Mariah felt the same way? And why the hell hadn't Ellie just broken up with me? Had she been scared of my reaction? I'd have never laid a hand on her in anger.

I'd let her go. I didn't even have to think about it. I'd sooner release her and let her find happiness elsewhere than tie her down and force her to live with me. I didn't give a shit what her dad or anyone else had to say about it. I wouldn't go through it again. I'd cost one woman her life already. I couldn't bear for the same thing to happen to Mariah.

No one knew about Ellie. I'd kept quiet, even when I'd been dating her. Not even when she'd died had I come clean to the club. She'd remained a part of my life, and only mine. Knowing I'd been the reason she ended it all had weighed heavy on me for a long time. I'd decided I wouldn't make a woman commit to me again. I'd intended to keep that vow, but I knew damn well if someone came along who'd sparked my interest, I'd have probably tried again.

It hadn't happened. Since Ellie, I'd never once found a woman I wanted to make my own. Then Casper had asked a favor of the club. He needed someone to claim Mariah. It hadn't been a hard decision. I'd seen right away no one else wanted to volunteer. I hadn't had anything to lose. No woman I wanted for my own, and after all this time, I knew I wouldn't find one.

I should have known it would blow up in my face.

I heard Mariah come out of her room. Part of me wanted to get up and check on her, but I also hesitated. I didn't want to push myself on her. Had our roles been reversed, I'd have wanted some space. So that's what I'd do. I'd let her roam the house and check things out. Closer to dinner, I'd check with her and see if she felt like eating or had any questions.

I scrubbed my hands up and down my face. How long would it take for her to accept her life was here with me? Or would she ever?

In any other situation, I'd have tossed her over my shoulder and pleasured her until she screamed. I'd have made sure she never wanted to leave my bed. But I couldn't exactly do that with a seventeen-year-old. I'd asked Farrah to decorate the guest room in preparation of her sister coming to live here. She'd chosen colors Mariah would like, but I hadn't thought to ask about other things. I had no idea what my woman enjoyed doing. Venom had brought a box of books for her. If she ran out of things to read, I figured she'd let me know.

"What the hell did I get myself into?" I muttered.

A knock sounded at my door, and I sat up. Had to be Mariah. She knocked again and I saw the knob turn. She pushed the door open and stood uncertainly in the hall. I motioned for her to enter, and she stepped inside.

"I'm sorry for the way I acted when I got here," she said.

I waved off her concern. "Not your fault, pretty girl. You didn't know what to expect. If anyone's sorry, it's me."

She came closer and stopped when our toes were nearly touching. "Why? What have you done to be sorry for?"

"I offered to claim you when Casper asked, but I didn't once consider how you'd react. It didn't even occur to me no one would tell you about the deal I'd made. I asked your sister to decorate the guest room last week, knowing it would be yours when you arrived. She knew you were mine. Your dad knew. Why didn't anyone tell you?"

She shrugged a shoulder. "I don't know. Either way, I'm here now and it seems I'm not leaving.

Shouldn't we make the best of the situation?"

I blanked my face so she wouldn't see how much her words had hurt. Make the best of it? It was Ellie all over again. Telling me what she must think I wanted to hear, but it clearly wasn't what Mariah actually wanted. If anything, it proved I should keep my distance, at least for a little while.

"I usually get a Prospect to pick up my groceries. If you'll make a list of things you like, I'll make sure to have the kitchen stocked for you. I don't have much in there right now. Would you want to order pizza?" I asked.

She gave a slight nod. "That's fine. Will you… will you eat with me?"

I gave her a half-smile. "Sure. You can pick a movie and we'll watch it while we eat."

"I take it my dad isn't coming back tonight?" she asked.

"Um, I don't know. He's visiting Farrah right now, and I think he plans to stay the night over there. Would you prefer to go to your sister's for dinner?"

She shook her head. "I'll visit her tomorrow. My dad clearly doesn't want to see me right now. I think it's best I keep my distance. He was so pissed. Guess I can't blame him. I had no idea what Ty was up to. How could I have been so stupid?"

I reached out and took her hand, lacing our fingers together for a brief moment. "You weren't stupid, Mariah. You thought he loved you."

She nodded. "I did. I should have known better. There had to be signs something was off. Like the fact he didn't want my family knowing we were seeing each other. Or not showing me the plane tickets. I bet my dad was right. I don't think there would have been a return ticket for me. Maybe he wasn't even taking me to Las Vegas. I wouldn't have known until it was too late."

"Come here," I said, reaching out to pull her closer. I wrapped my arms around her, hugging her tight. "You had no reason to think he was lying to you. Any guy would be lucky to be loved by you. I know I'm not who you wanted, but I promise you'll be safe with me. And for the record, the moment I agreed to claim you, I gave up seeing any other women. I've been faithful to you, even though you didn't know about me yet."

She pulled back a little, her cheeks turning pink. "I, um… With Ty, I mean, we…"

I took a breath and gave her another smile. "It's all right, Mariah. But from this point forward, you're mine. No more guys, okay?"

"All right."

It was a start. Not perfect, but I'd take it. We'd muddle along best we could, and when she'd gotten a little older, I'd make her mine in all ways. Until then, we'd have to figure out how to live together. I had a feeling I was in for a bumpy road.

Chapter Three

Mariah
Three Months Later

The second *Scream* movie started as I stretched out on the couch. After night had fallen, I'd decided on a movie marathon, hoping it would keep my mind busy. It hadn't escaped my notice Savage seemed to be avoiding me. He wasn't cruel about it, but I didn't understand. He'd claimed *me*, not the other way around. If he hadn't wanted me here, why bother?

It shouldn't have hurt. We were still strangers for the most part. Except… the times I'd been around him, the little bit I'd learned about him, made me realize he was a genuinely good guy. It didn't hurt he was also extremely sexy, especially for a guy twice my age. I'd caught him shirtless a few times, and those images had haunted my dreams. He didn't have huge bulging muscles. Honestly, I'd never found those men to be attractive. But his chest and abs had enough definition I'd wanted to run my fingers over them. And his arms… I fanned my face. Yeah, I could admit it. I was an arm woman. My sister called it arm porn, and she wasn't wrong.

I pulled the throw pillow over my face and groaned in frustration. I didn't know how to get Savage's attention. The man treated me like a roommate. Case in point, he'd ducked out after breakfast this morning and hadn't come back. All I'd gotten was a text saying he'd be home late. Not a single text or call all day other than that.

I threw the pillow aside and stared at the ceiling, thinking about Sidney's PG-13 relationship in the first *Scream*. "I'd take one of those right now. Better than *no* relationship."

Sighing, I got up off the couch and decided I needed more junk food. Popcorn and brownies made everything better, right? On the plus side, I'd been teaching myself to cook and bake since I'd been here. It wasn't like I had a lot of other ways to kill time. I didn't see the point in going to college when most of the old ladies I'd known didn't work. Sure, I could have gotten a pretty piece of paper saying I'd earned a degree, but what the hell would I do with it?

While the popcorn popped, I leaned against the counter and shut my eyes. This morning, Savage had been in this exact spot. His jeans had ridden low on his hips, and his T-shirt had molded to him. What would it feel like to have him cage me in against the counter? I'd seen Demon do that to Farrah, and my dad was always after my mom.

I could almost feel the heat of his body, smell the cologne he preferred. A whimper slipped past my lips as I shifted my weight, feeling all hot and achy. I slid my hands up my ribs to cup my breasts, flicking my nipples and wishing it was Savage touching me. My panties dampened and I started to slip my hand inside my sleep shorts, but the beeping of the microwave broke the spell.

Pushing away from the counter, I turned to open the microwave and froze. My gaze clashed with a set of green eyes. I blinked, wondering who the hell was standing outside the kitchen window. Between the light in the kitchen and how dark it was outside, his face wasn't clear. The man slowly backed away, blending into the night. I gripped the edge of the counter wondering just what he'd seen. I'd had my back to the window. He hadn't known what I was doing, had he?

My cheeks warmed. I yanked the popcorn from

the microwave and nearly dropped it, not thinking about how hot it would be. I poured it into a large bowl, snagged a brownie off the plate on the counter, and got a cold drink before going back to my movie marathon. Even though I had no idea who had been spying on me, I figured it had to be either a Prospect or patched member for the club. They didn't let just anyone wander into their territory.

I sat on the couch and ate my treats, trying not to think about how much I wanted Savage to notice me. I'd tried a few times to make myself come, wanting to take the edge off, but it never worked. My fingers weren't enough to get the job done, and yet I still tried at least once a week.

After I'd gotten so full I thought I might pop, I set the leftovers aside and stretched out again. My phone rang and I saw my mother's name flash across the screen. I answered, knowing she'd just keep calling if I didn't.

"Hey, Mom," I said as I accepted the call.

"Um."

I blinked a moment. "Dawson?"

My little brother cleared his throat. "I borrowed Mom's phone."

"And does she know you borrowed it?"

"Not exactly," he mumbled. "You left without saying goodbye and you've been gone forever."

My heart ached at his words. I'd been so angry with my dad I hadn't even thought about giving Dawson a hug before I'd left. Now I felt like utter shit about it.

"I'm sorry, D. I didn't mean to run off without saying bye."

"Dad and Mom have been arguing a lot." He dropped his voice a little lower to a near whisper. "I hear your name when they start screaming. Did you do something wrong? Is that why Dad made you leave?"

I closed my eyes and wondered how much I should tell him. There were times Dawson seemed much older than his years, and then there was now, when I had to remember he was just a little kid.

"It's complicated, D. Dad found out who I'd been dating, and he got mad. He never told me I'd already been promised to someone. I live at the Devil's Fury compound now, like Farrah."

His voice perked up a little. "Really? So you're an old lady now?"

I didn't feel much like one. More like a nuisance. "Yep. I have a property cut and everything."

"That's so cool! I'm going to have a cut one day."

I smiled. "Yeah? Want to be a Dixie Reaper like Dad?"

"Nope. I'm going to move there with you and Farrah. Then we can all be together."

I laughed silently, knowing my dad would just love that. I only hoped I got to be there when Dawson told him. I missed my little brother, and my parents. Being at the Devil's Fury wasn't awful by any means, but it was a bit lonely. Farrah stayed busy, as did the other old ladies, and I didn't have transportation to go out and make new friends outside the club. I'd tried talking to some of the Prospects. It hadn't ended well. I had a feeling they worried Savage would go after them, but he'd have to care and I didn't think he did.

"I better go before Mom looks for her phone," Dawson said. "Love you, Riah."

"Love you too, little brother. You can call me anytime. And if Mom won't let you use her phone, just ask for your own."

He snickered. "Like she's going to get me one

anytime soon. I'll probably have to get a job and buy my own."

After telling him bye one more time, I hung up and sighed. I hadn't realized how much I needed to hear his voice until just then. I wondered when I'd get a chance to visit, or if my parents would bring him here sometime.

The front door opened and softly clicked shut. I stood and took a hesitant step toward the front entry. Savage appeared just outside the living room, and I wondered if he'd acknowledge me or keep going. He'd slicked his hair back with water, which made me think he'd taken a shower. Clearly not at home, so where?

My stomach soured as I thought about him being with another woman. Had he taken one of the club whores into a room at the clubhouse? Or did he have a girlfriend somewhere? When I'd found out he'd claimed he, he'd assured me he hadn't touched anyone since that day. I'd believed him, but now... The longer he treated me like an unwanted guest, the more I had to feel like he had someone else in his life. I'd never heard of my dad's club, or the ones they considered allies, ever ditching their old ladies, or being unfaithful to them. But there was always a first time, right?

He paused and slowly turned his head my way. "Thought you'd be in bed by now."

I glanced at the time on my phone. Nearly midnight. I'd been watching movies longer than I'd thought. Why had Dawson been calling me so late? My brow furrowed thinking he'd called for a reason other than to say hi and that he missed me, and now it would bug me until I found out. I didn't dare call my mom's phone so late. If I did, I'd have to tell her I'd just spoken with Dawson, and I didn't want to get him into trouble.

"Something wrong?" he asked, stepping into the room.

"No. At least, I don't think so. I got a call from my little brother, not realizing what time it was, and now I'm wondering why he really called. At this time of night he had to feel it was important."

"Think it's something to do with your parents? Or the club?" Savage asked.

I shrugged a shoulder, having no idea. I did wonder if he'd reached out to Farrah too, but I wasn't about to call her. With a little one at home, she could very well be sleeping by now.

"What do you want to do?" Savage asked.

"Nothing right now. If I call Mom, she'll know Dawson used her phone to call me. She may anyway if she checks the call history. I don't want to get him into trouble if it's not important. I can try to call him tomorrow."

Savage pulled out his phone and tapped on the screen for a minute. He cracked his neck and stared at the device until it chimed, his eyebrows going up.

"What?" I asked.

"Farrah didn't hear from Dawson, but she did hear from Danica. It seems Chief Daniels is cleaning house, which he mentioned to his daughter."

I nodded. "And then Hayley told Danica. Why would Dawson call me over that?"

"Because the cops in question are pissed as fuck. The chief couldn't arrest anyone other than Officer Clarke, but he thinks the guy has an accomplice within the department. I think your little brother overheard something and got worried about you."

I chewed my lower lip. Right, because if Ty did have a partner, he'd know I was the reason everything blew up. They had to have realized they couldn't sell the kid of a Dixie Reaper. How stupid were they? Once I'd gone missing, my dad would have torn the world apart trying to find me. No one had known I'd been dating Ty, but there was a chance someone in town had seen us together. My dad had clearly set up something with Savage before the day I'd been hauled here, which meant he'd suspected if he hadn't known outright.

"What's bothering you, Mariah? You know I'll keep you safe."

"It's not that. If Ty did have a partner, they had to know he planned to sell me. Then I go missing and not long after, Ty gets arrested for human trafficking? They aren't complete idiots, even if they were dumb enough to target a Dixie Reaper's daughter." He motioned for me to keep going, since I clearly hadn't gotten to the point yet. "It made me realize my dad had to have set up something with you before the day we arrived. You'd known ahead of time I was yours, even if no one had told me. So it made me think my dad knew all along I'd been seeing Ty."

"I don't know when he figured it out," Savage said. "But yeah, he knew before that day. I'm not sure why he waited so long to bring you here. I'd thought it would be immediately, but then a week passed."

"I think they were all working on the mess with Danica and that rodeo guy," I said. "I know Dad was pretty busy that week."

"Could be." Savage shoved his hands into his pockets. "Were you having a movie marathon?"

"Yeah. *Scream.* I only made it through the first two. I'm honestly not tired so I may watch the third one." I nervously tucked my hair behind my ear. "Did you want to watch it with me?"

He rocked back on his heels and shook his head.

"Probably not the best idea. It's been a long day. Think I'll head to bed."

Right. I sighed and went back to the couch, knowing that was the end of it. He'd vanish into his room, and I wouldn't see him again until morning. Was it so wrong I wanted to spend time with him? I wanted to feel his arms around me, press against his side while we cuddled on the couch, and maybe get him to finally kiss me. It seemed it wouldn't be happening anytime soon, if ever. His rejection hurt, especially with all the doubts swirling through my mind. Who claimed someone and then avoided them? Did he find me unattractive?

Oh, God! That had to be it. He wasn't attracted to me even a little and didn't know how to tell me. Or maybe he couldn't stand the thought of touching me and just planned to keep me prisoner here because he'd given his word to my dad's club. I curled into a ball in the corner of the couch and blankly stared at the screen as I heard his booted steps moving farther away.

Tears burned my eyes, but I didn't dare cry. The Dixie Reapers might not allow women to patch in, but as far as I was concerned I was a Reaper by blood, and a Dixie Reaper didn't cry. Besides, if Savage didn't want me and was too big of a chickenshit to just tell me, then he didn't deserve my tears, or another second of my time.

So why did the thought of never truly being his hurt so much?

* * *

Savage

I leaned back against my closed door and scrubbed my hands over my face. What the fuck was I going to do? The longer I had Mariah in my house, the harder it was to keep my distance. I snorted, staring down at my cock trying to push through my zipper. Maybe *harder* hadn't been the best choice of words. I didn't know for sure if she'd had a birthday yet, and I wasn't about to touch her if she hadn't.

I wasn't a saint by any stretch of the imagination. Hell, I'd borrowed Colorado's shower after working on a car with him. And I'd made sure it was ice-cold, hoping it would help when I came home. Just the thought of Mariah was enough to get me hard most days. But tonight? Shit. The shirt she'd been wearing barely covered her breasts, and the shorts looked more like underwear. Didn't help I'd asked Garrick to make sure she was all right, and he'd caught her touching herself. Or he said it's what he'd thought she was doing.

I closed my eyes, picturing her bent over in those, and the way they'd ride up, showing off the lower part of her ass cheeks. Groaning, I reached for my belt and started unfastening my pants. No fucking way I'd get any sleep if I didn't take the edge off. Wouldn't do much good. The second I heard her, smelled her, or thought about her, I'd be sporting wood again.

I toed off my boots and removed my clothes. I'd already had a shower, but I damn sure didn't want her to hear me and know what I was doing. I already felt like a fucking pervert. I went into the bathroom and started the water, then braced my hands on the counter and stared at my reflection.

What did Mariah think when she looked at me? Sometimes I couldn't tell. Then again, I'd done my best to avoid eye contact. I knew there were roughly two decades between us. Plenty of people would see us and assume I had my daughter with me, or if they realized she was my woman, I'd get disgusted looks. My attraction to her went beyond her looks, though. The little bit of time I'd spent around her, I'd learned she had a good sense of humor, a sharp wit, and she genuinely cared about other people.

I fucking hated the asshole cop had gotten to her, made her fall for him, then spewed a bunch of lies all over her, luring her in. She'd fallen into his trap, and I kept asking myself why. Most of those girls had been missing something in their lives. Some had absent parents or didn't have friends. I knew the Dixie Reapers loved Mariah. She had both family and friends within the club, and their protection. So what had Officer Clarke offered that she couldn't get anywhere else?

She'd mentioned how he'd been sweet to her, taking her on dates, making her feel special. Had that been it? She didn't feel special enough outside her relationship with him? If that was the case, I knew I was fucking shit up with her. But I couldn't give her the time she wanted, without getting a noticeable erection. The last thing I wanted was for her to feel like she *had* to sleep with me. Yeah, I'd claimed her, but I wasn't about to force her into my bed.

I pushed away from the sink, not caring too much for the man looking back at me, and I got into the shower. My dick still pointed up, even with all my thoughts about how Mariah had ended up here. I reached for the soap and poured some into my palm before gripping my shaft. Using long, slow strokes, I decided to enjoy the build-up. Maybe it would keep me soft longer once I was done.

I leaned back against the tiled wall and shut my eyes, picturing Mariah in the shower with me.

The water cascaded off her body, beading on her breasts. A sultry smile spread across her lips as she curled her fingers around my cock. I let her tease me, enjoying the heat in her eyes. My dick jerked in her hand and I growled, spinning her to face the wall. I caged her in with my body, letting my hands cup her breasts.

Her nipples beaded against my palms, and I pinched her nipples, giving them a slight pull. She gasped and pressed back against me. I loved how much she wanted me, needed my touch. I slid my hands down her sides, over her hips, then worked one between her legs. She clamped her thighs tight, not letting me in.

I bit down on her shoulder, just enough to sting, and kicked her legs apart, knowing she enjoyed this part of our game. She always pretended not to want it, when I knew the second I touched her pussy she'd be soaking wet. I spread her lips and ran my fingers over her clit before plunging two inside her.

"Yes! Savage, please... I need to come!"

I worked her pussy and rubbed my cock against her ass. The second I felt her coming, I pulled my fingers free and shoved my cock into her. She cried out, her pussy gripping me tight, as I fucked her against the shower wall. Her cream coated me as I drove into her, not stopping until she'd come twice. I felt my balls draw up and grunted as my release spurted inside her.

My hips kept thrusting until every drop of cum had been wrung from my balls. The woman completely undid me, every damn time.

I panted for breath, opening my eyes. My cum slid down the opposite wall and I groaned, wishing it hadn't been a fantasy. I had several, but that one always got me to come the hardest. I cleaned up the shower and myself. By the time I'd finished, my dick was already getting hard again. I shook my head, wondering what it would take to go soft and stay that way for a while. Never thought I'd be bitching about having a quick recovery time, especially at my age.

"Fucking hell, Mariah. What am I going to do about you?" I mumbled.

I couldn't remember the last time I'd been so attracted to someone. I hadn't even felt like this with Ellie. When it came to Mariah, I thought about her all the fucking time, and wanted to spend every second of the day with her. I couldn't, but I wanted to. Being around her too much would possibly snap my control, and I'd never forgive myself if I hurt her or scared her in any way.

After I dried off and tossed the towel into the hamper, I slid into bed and pulled the sheet over me. I'd always slept naked until Mariah arrived. Those first few weeks, I'd at least kept my underwear on in case she needed me. Not once had she called out to me or tried to come find me at night. So I'd gone back to my habit of not wearing anything to bed. I hated feeling confined when I slept.

I didn't know how long I could avoid Mariah. I left the house every day and stayed gone most nights until I thought she might be in bed. If I didn't see her, I wouldn't be tempted. I might have thought her skimpy clothes were a cry for my attention, but she knew I wouldn't be here to see whatever outfit she'd chosen. Hell, for all I knew, those were her pajamas.

I groaned, throwing my arm over my eyes. Great. Now I wondered if she wore that to bed, or if she preferred to sleep without clothes. Maybe she had one of those slinky, sexy nightgowns some women liked. I'd never seen her do laundry and had no idea what she'd brought with her or bought, for that matter. I'd attached my credit card to some of the apps on her phone, and she hadn't overspent so far.

At first, I'd looked at the receipts to see where she'd been shopping, but it looked like she mostly bought books. A few places sold clothes and shoes, but it wasn't like I got an itemized list of what she purchased. There was so much I wanted to know about her, and yet I didn't dare ask. Since I'd claimed her as my old lady, I had every right to ask her whatever I wanted. Didn't mean I felt comfortable doing it.

"How the fuck did I go from having women throw themselves at me to being a damn pussy when it comes to my own woman? My brothers would laugh their asses off," I mumbled to myself.

I tensed when a soft knock sounded at the door.

"Savage?" Mariah called out. "Are you asleep already?"

I got up and wrapped the sheet around my waist before I answered the door. Her lips parted as she scanned me from head to toe. Before I realized what the hell I was doing, I found myself flexing a little. Fuck me. Not having sex was starting to rot my fucking brain and kill any common sense I'd had.

"Something wrong, Mariah?" I asked.

She licked her lips, dragging her gaze back up to my eyes. "Um, I... Uh..."

I smirked and waited. Good to know she wasn't unaffected. It made me feel a little better about getting myself off in the shower every day, sometimes more than once.

"I wanted to know if you'd be here for breakfast," she said softly.

I started to say no, until I saw the hope shining in her eyes. Hell. I couldn't be that big of a bastard to her. "Yeah, baby girl. I'll be here."

She smiled, her cheeks flushing. "Good. I found a new recipe for some banana walnut pancakes. I've been wanting to try it, but it makes far too much for just me."

"Sounds great." She started to back away, then stopped, shifting from one foot to the other. "Did you need something else?"

"What about lunch or dinner? I could make whatever you want. You haven't told me all your favorite dishes yet."

Did she want me to be here for those meals? Was this her somewhat subtle way of asking me to spend more time with her? It wouldn't hurt to enjoy a few meals with her. Not every day or I'd lose my fucking mind, but I could handle at least two meals tomorrow.

"I'll stay for breakfast and be back by dinner. If you want, we can have dinner in the living room and watch a movie."

"I'd like that," she said softly. "Thanks, Savage."

I watched her walk down the hall to her room, admiring the sway of her hips and the roundness of her ass. And now my cock was hard again. Perfect.

I shut the door and locked it before going back to bed. Except this time I grabbed the box of tissues and the tube of lube I kept in the drawer. Looked like I needed to relieve a little more tension before I tried to sleep. The woman was killing me. I hadn't yanked one out as frequently as I had in the last few months since I'd been a teenager. Granted, back then I'd been sleeping with Ellie. Just wished I'd known she hadn't wanted to and had felt obligated.

My cock softened a little. At least I now knew how to get rid of an erection. Just think of my ex and the fucked-up shit I'd found out, far too late for it to matter.

Chapter Four

Mariah
Nine Months Later

"I've underestimated him," I said, as I reached for another brownie. My sister pursed her lips and seemed to be every bit as confused as me.

"He knows you're eighteen now, right?" she asked.

I shrugged a shoulder. I hadn't made a huge deal about my birthday. In fact, Savage hadn't given me a present, or even said *happy birthday* to me. In the last week, it honestly hadn't occurred to me he may not have known I'd had a birthday since moving in with him. I'd been so busy wearing skimpy clothes and doing my best to seduce him, I'd forgotten the most important part... making sure he knew I'd turned eighteen. It had been a year since I'd arrived at the Devil's Fury. Surely the man could do basic math?

Farrah snatched the half-eaten brownie from my hand. "Seriously, Mariah? You live with the man, and you never thought to let him know about your birthday?"

"Well, you did bring a cake over. My favorite." I reached over and took my brownie back, shoving the entire thing in my mouth before she could steal it again. Then proceeded to mumble around it, which I knew she hated. "I didn't realize I needed to make an announcement."

Farrah narrowed her eyes. "I didn't understand a word of that, and you damn well know it. Not to mention -- gross!"

I flipped her off and guzzled some soda to wash down the brownie. "I said... I didn't realize I needed to make an announcement. I've been here exactly twelve months. He knew I was seventeen when I got here. The man isn't stupid. He has to have realized I turned eighteen since moving in with him."

Farrah opened and shut her mouth, shaking her head. "No, he really doesn't have to realize it. Haven't you learned anything? These guys have tunnel vision at times. And birthdays? They tend to get overlooked unless you drop hints. And I don't mean subtle ones."

I heard a growl and realized my brother-in-law had found us, or more accurately he'd found his woman and the brownies. If Demon didn't scare me so bad, I'd smack his hand when he reached for two of the delicious treats. "Only tunnel vision I have is when you're naked."

I slapped my hand over my face. "Really? I don't need to think about you and my sister having sex. That's just... No. A million times, no."

"Why are you here?" he asked. "Don't you have anything better to do?"

And therein lay the problem. No. I really didn't. I sighed and grabbed one more brownie before standing up. "I can tell when I'm not wanted. But for the record, I finished my last year of high school online shortly after I got here. I don't have transportation. No friends. Didn't sign up for college classes. No job. So no, I don't have jack shit to do around here."

I chomped into the chocolatey goodness in my hand and trudged out of their kitchen. Since my dad had brought everything of mine, except my car, I walked back to the house, trying to think of a way to get Savage's attention. There were days I thought I'd become invisible. He'd assured me he hadn't touched a woman since he'd claimed me, even if he didn't take advantage of the fact I belonged to him, but I had to wonder... had he kept his promise since I'd arrived?

Twelve months was a long-ass time to be celibate, or so I'd assume. Since I'd never had sex, going without might be a bit frustrating, but it wasn't like I'd ever tasted the forbidden fruit.

I passed Rachel and Steel, smiling at the sight of the older man playing with his kids in the front yard. I gave them a wave and kept walking, knowing if I stopped I'd end up spilling my guts, and it wasn't a conversation to be had in front of children. If Farrah and Demon's evil spawn, Rebel, had been home, I wouldn't have been talking to my sister about it either. My nearly two-year-old niece had more of a social life than I did. Every week she went to Wolf's house to play with his daughter, Sienna.

Frustration bubbled inside me as I walked up to the house. Savage's bike wasn't under the carport, which meant he was most likely at the clubhouse. Unless he had a girlfriend. A sharp pain stabbed me right in my heart at the thought of him with another woman. I knew he slept here every night, but it didn't mean he didn't run off during the day to visit someone else's bed, especially since he avoided mine like I had the damn plague.

I needed a distraction. Something to take my mind off the fact Savage had clearly lost interest in me, assuming he'd ever wanted me to begin with. Would I always be a kid in his eyes? What had been the point of him claiming me if he never planned to touch me? I'd be damned if I was going to die a virgin!

I hadn't even realized I'd been standing in the driveway staring at the stupid house until I heard someone come up behind me. I heard a bike turn off as I turned, and I mustered a smile. Or I tried to.

"Bad day?" the Prospect asked.

"Yeah. Feeling sorry for myself." I shook my

head. "I know I could have it a lot worse. Some days are just harder than others."

He opened his mouth, then shut it. I had to wonder what he'd been about to say. With a shake of his head and a quick wave, he drove off.

I fisted my hands, threw back my head, and screamed as long and loud as I could. What the hell was wrong with the men around here? Afterward, I felt marginally better. I went into the house, only to freeze and wonder what I would do with myself. The place was already spotless. I could only watch so much TV before it felt like my brain would rot. I'd read every book I had in the house.

I paced the length of the living room. I felt like a prisoner. Without a car, I couldn't leave the compound. I didn't have a job, so I didn't have money of my own. Savage had let me add his card to a few apps on my phone so I could find things to read, listen to, or watch. I'd refrained from buying anything too expensive, not having any idea what his finances were like.

"Fuck it," I muttered, yanking my phone from my pocket. "He wants to leave me here, all caged up, then he can deal with the consequences. He wants to ignore me? Fine. I'll make it damn impossible for him to pretend I'm not here."

I started scrolling through a shopping app, deciding what I should buy. After adding two throw pillows for the couch, a rug for the front entry, half a dozen candles, and a few framed prints, I stopped and wondered exactly how bad I should be. Two months ago, I'd walked into Farrah's house in the middle of what appeared to be an online sex toy party of some sort. I'd been all kinds of embarrassed and left immediately. Now I wished I'd stayed.

Savage didn't want to touch me? Very well. I'd

just have to give myself orgasms instead. I'd tried multiple times but using my fingers didn't do anything for me. I pulled up the adult toys in the app and tried to decide what I wanted to buy. Since I'd never used any, I had no idea what I'd like.

"So just buy a variety," I muttered to myself, then added four toys to the shopping cart. By the time I checked out, my total had risen to nearly seven hundred dollars. All but two items on the list were available for same day delivery. There was no way Savage wouldn't notice a new rug and the throw pillows, right?

My finger hesitated over the payment button. Part of me felt bad. I had no idea if spending so much would hurt Savage financially. Then there was the other part... the side tired of being ignored. Before I could chicken out, I pressed *pay now*. My palms were sweating, and I wondered if Savage would notice right away, or if he even kept track of the bank account. For that matter, I didn't even know if the card I'd just used was a debit card or a regular credit card.

What the hell had I just done?

I didn't know which Prospect guarded the gate today, but it clearly wasn't Van. Savage had me program every patched member and each Prospect into my phone the day after I'd arrived. I didn't know why Van, Talbot, and Garrick hadn't patched in already, but I knew the club had their reasons. Then again, it had been really quiet. Maybe they hadn't had a way to prove themselves yet.

I called Talbot first.

"Hello?" he answered, sounding hesitant, like he didn't know who had called him. Did no one add my number to their phones? It wasn't like I'd never called the guy before.

"It's Mariah. Are you on the gate today?"

"For another hour. Did you need something? I can ask Garrick or Van to run it over to you, whatever it is."

"No, nothing like that. I ordered some stuff and it's being delivered today. It's probably going to be a rather large load since one of the items is a rug."

"If it's not here before I leave, I'll let Garrick know. He's up next," Talbot said. "We'll use one of the club trucks to haul everything to your house."

"Thanks, Tal."

I ended the call and hoped like hell everything got here before Savage came home. I wanted to see how long it took him to realize anything around the house looked different. Assuming he noticed at all. I still remembered the time my mother threw out all the dishes and bought new ones. It had taken my dad nearly a month to notice, and they'd been completely different.

I felt almost giddy about my first adult purchases. Or more accurately, my first sex toys. I'd overheard my sister talking about what she claimed was an amazing vibrator and I'd been curious ever since. Not enough to actually buy one. Until now. If Savage didn't want to touch me, then I'd just have to give myself orgasms.

I folded my arms and stared out the living room window, wondering again where he disappeared to every day. The first few days I'd been here, he'd been nice. Maybe not super attentive, but he'd listened when I talked, and he'd introduced me to the club. I'd met a few of them already through Farrah, but it had been different when Savage introduced me as his old lady.

I snorted. Old lady, my ass! More like unwanted

houseguest. If I had anywhere else to go, I'd leave. Then again, I'd need a car in order to pull that off. My dad had made sure I couldn't run away. When he'd first left me here, he'd been right to be worried. With Officer Clarke on the loose, and apparently planning to sell me to the highest bidder, I'd needed to remain locked behind the gates. As the months passed, even though Officer Clarke had been taken into custody, I'd given up hope he'd ever bring my car to me. I hadn't had the heart to ask my mom if he'd sold it.

Things needed to change. I couldn't keep living in this house, feeling like an inconvenience to Savage. Hell, my own sister hardly had time for me. I understood Farrah had a family of her own now. Didn't make it hurt any less. I'd never felt so isolated before. Back home, I'd had friends both in the club and outside it.

A knock at the door pulled me from my melancholy thoughts. I rushed to answer it, giving the Prospect a smile as he started to haul my packages into the house. It didn't take long for me to set out my new things and carry the toys to my bathroom. I washed them, set the waterproof one in the shower, and decided I'd have a little fun while I waited for Savage to come home. The others needed to charge, and I'd have to figure out where I'd plug them in. The one for the shower took batteries, and I quickly added them, having ordered a few sizes when I'd gone shopping online. It never hurt to keep batteries stocked.

Excitement rushed through me as I turned on the water, letting it warm while I stripped out of my clothes. I stuck my hand under the spray, testing the temperature, then made sure I'd shut the bathroom door before I climbed in. I soaked my hair and washed my body as I eyed the toy.

I reached for the vibrator and switched it on, jumping a little as it whirred to life in my hand. I'd never seen one up close before. The texture felt more rubbery than I'd expected. I'd ordered a variety. Some were smooth, one was a hard plastic, and I'd even bought a glass dildo.

"Here goes nothing," I murmured to myself.

I leaned back against the shower wall and spread my thighs a little. Placing the buzzing toy against my clit, I gasped and my eyes went wide. My legs shook and I couldn't hold back the keening sound that escaped me as I came for the first time in my life. The bathroom door slammed into the wall before I had a chance to catch my breath and a large hand gripped the shower curtain, yanking it open. I gaped at Savage, who looked every bit as wild and fierce as his name suggested.

"Baby girl, you are in so much trouble." He narrowed his eyes on me before scanning the room and taking in all the toys I'd bought.

Well, I'd wanted his attention. Looked like I had it now.

* * *

Savage

I'd thought I must have been mistaken. Little Mariah wasn't in the shower getting herself off. Except she'd been doing exactly that. She'd been teasing me for months, and now she thought she could orgasm while I wasn't even home? Fuck that! I stared her down as she gave me a deer in the headlights look.

"Who gave you permission to make yourself come? Or to order all these toys?" I demanded. I should have paid closer attention to what she'd been buying, but hell, she hadn't asked me for a damn thing.

It hadn't seemed right to put a limit on her spending.

She gasped and folded her hands over her breasts as her cheeks flamed a bright pink. The little vibrator buzzed against her, but she didn't seem to notice. "I don't need permission. It's my body."

I leaned closer. "Wrong, baby girl. You're mine. Every single inch of you belongs to me. I'm starting to see why the Dixie Reapers ink their women. You need a more permanent reminder than my name across your back on a property cut?"

I could see her pulse racing. I also noticed her eyes dilated when I said she belonged to me. I'd been fighting my attraction to her. I knew she had to be eighteen by now, even though she'd not said a damn word about her birthday. But at forty-one I'd already lived my life, made mistakes, and had some fun along the way. I'd tried to give her some space and a bit of time to adjust and settle into her new life here. It seemed I'd fucked up.

"You don't get to say I belong to you when you've ignored me for a year." She dropped her hands, and the toy, and glared at me. "You can't have it both ways, Savage. I'm either yours, or I'm just an unwanted houseguest. In which case, give me transportation and I'll get out of your way."

Unwanted houseguest? Unwanted?

I growled and leaned into the shower. I shut the water off before gripping her arms with my hands and yanking her out. I'd show her exactly how much I wanted her. She didn't resist as I lifted her onto the bathroom counter. If anything, she thrust her breasts up, as if she didn't already have my undivided attention. Little cocktease!

"That what you think? I don't want you?" I asked.

She tipped her chin up. "You haven't acted like
you do. You barely speak to me. The second you've
had breakfast, you run from the house and stay gone
all day. Even when we do spend time together, it's like
we're not even in the same room. There's an invisible
wall between us."

How the fuck had I read everything so wrong?
I'd been staying away, not wanting to move too fast,
and instead I'd ended up pissing her off. Yeah, she'd
been flirting and wearing skimpy things, but I hadn't
thought too much of it. I'd thought she'd been seeing if
she could push me, test the boundaries so to speak.
Instead, she'd desperately wanted my attention.

"A wall? You think I've put up a barrier between
us? You saying you don't want anything between us?
And think carefully before you answer, Mariah."

She stared at me, and I could see the thoughts
flitting through her mind. Even though I'd made her
my old lady, I wouldn't force her to be mine in all
ways. I'd thought she might need some time to grow
up, spread her wings a little, before being ready to go
all in. And if she couldn't ever be my old lady in truth,
then I'd be discreet and ask the same of her. She'd be
mine in the eyes of my club and others, but I'd never
forced myself on a woman and I wouldn't start now.

I sighed at her hesitation. This had been the
reason I hadn't acted on my desire for her. Hell, I'd
been hard for the past year, even when I had no right
to think of her as anything more than a teen girl.
Except she'd been right that first day. The age of
consent in Georgia was sixteen. I'd still decided I
wouldn't so much as kiss her until she'd turned
eighteen. Didn't need anyone up in arms, claiming I
was a child molester or some shit. I didn't see the
difference in a handful of months between the time

she'd arrived and when I thought she'd had her birthday. Then I'd realized I didn't know when her damn birthday was and I'd felt like a fucking idiot, so I hadn't asked her. If I'd talked to Farrah or Demon, it would have gotten back to Mariah. Shouldn't I know my woman's birthday?

"You know I'd never force you, right?" I asked, holding her gaze. "Your dad didn't really give you a choice. Just dropped you here and said you were mine. You know the way things work with the clubs. Doesn't mean I'll make you stay with me, or demand you share my bed. If you want to walk, tell me now."

Her lips parted and her breath caught for a moment. It even seemed her eyes were getting glassy. What the fuck? Was she about to cry?

"Is that why you haven't touched me? You thought you'd have to force me? Or are you *hoping* I'll ask to walk away?" Her lips trembled and I knew I'd fucking lose it if she started bawling.

"No, pretty girl. I kept my distance because I thought I was doing the right thing. For you. You hadn't asked for any of this, and I wanted you to have time to settle in, get to know people, figure out your place with the Devil's Fury. Maybe make new friends."

She gave a soft snort. "I can't make friends when I can't leave the compound, and everyone is always busy. The others have children, even my sister, so it's not like I've had anyone to hang out with the last year."

My gaze dropped to her chest and I shifted, trying to ease the ache of my hard cock pressing against my zipper. "Maybe we need to have this discussion with more clothes on."

She looked away, but not before I caught the flash of pain in her eyes. I reached out and gently nudged her chin so she'd face me. She looked so... defeated. Not at all like the little spitfire who'd arrived on my doorstep with Venom. Had I done this to her? Fuck me. I'd screwed up more than I'd realized.

The damn toy in the tub still buzzed, annoying the fuck out of me and pissing me off all over again. I couldn't believe she'd been trying to get herself off while I'd been walking around with my dick hard for a damn year.

Making a decision, one I hoped neither of us regretted, I lifted her into my arms and carried her to my bedroom. I kicked the door open with my booted foot and eased her down onto the unmade bed. Then I started to strip. I stopped when I got down to my underwear and nudged her over.

Tugging her into my arms, I yanked the covers over us, and decided to hold her while we had a long overdue conversation. And if my dick had ideas about ending up in her pussy, well that was for me to know.

Mariah cuddled against me, and I felt her trembling. I ran my hand down her hip and upper thigh, then back up to her ribs before stroking the same way again. It took a moment, but she inhaled sharply, then started to relax as she exhaled.

"I never intended to make you feel alone," I said. "I thought I was doing the right thing. If you'd wanted me around, you should have said something."

"You didn't give me a chance."

I winced, knowing she was right. I'd fled the house as fast as I could every day, simply because being near her was too damn hard. Or rather, being near her *made* me hard. She might have come on to me that first day, but I'd assumed she'd done it to get a rise out of me or her dad. Even the flirting she'd done had seemed more innocent than her trying to get in my pants. Then again, I hadn't taken into consideration her age. She'd mentioned she'd been with Officer Clarke. I'd assumed it meant she'd been with him sexually, and there could have been others. Why the fuck hadn't someone said anything to me? Her sister had to have known how she felt.

"I'm sorry. I promised you were safe with me, and unintentionally, I hurt you. I hadn't just meant your physical safety. I let you down, but it won't happen again. Not if you give me a chance to make things right."

She snuggled closer. "You really don't want me to leave?"

"No, pretty girl. I don't. I've been so damn hard for months, wanting you in my bed, but worried you weren't ready."

"I appreciate you trying to be so thoughtful, Savage, but what I needed and wanted was for you to be here. I wanted to get to know you. Build some sort of relationship."

"So let's start now." She started to shake, and I realized she was silently laughing at me. "Why is that funny?"

"Because I'm naked, you're nearly naked, and we're in your bed. Are you sure you're wanting to get to know me in a way that doesn't include you fucking me?"

I glowered down at her. "What the hell, Mariah?"

"Just sayin'. What sort of conversation did you plan to have with my boobs pressed against you?"

I blinked and tried hard not to think about the fact every naked of inch of her molded to me. She had a point, though. If I'd wanted to have a serious talk, I should have kept my clothes on. And insisted she put some on too. But the look in her eyes, the way she'd thought I didn't want her, it had made me want to prove her wrong. Even now, my dick tented the sheets.

"I guess the kind where I proved you aren't unwanted," I said, waving a hand to my cock. "Then you made the excellent point we should have spent the last year getting to know one another. So I started to rethink my strategy."

"For the longest time I've worried you had a girlfriend," she said. "The way you always took off and stayed gone all day... I didn't know what else to think. I'd been around Farrah enough times to know Demon didn't leave all day every day. It's part of why I haven't spent a lot of time with her. That and their kid."

"Rebel is a good reason to run." I smiled. "She's something else."

"What were they thinking?" she asked. "Rebel? Seriously? It's like they jinxed themselves. Bad enough she's the product of Demon and my wild sister. That poor girl didn't stand a chance."

I rubbed her hip again. "Do you want kids? Maybe not right this minute, but someday?"

"Yeah, I do. As for when, I always thought it would happen when it was supposed to. I'm not on birth control, and I hadn't planned to start it once I got married. I always believed life doesn't give us more than we can handle."

"You've been around the Devil's Boneyard before. Can you honestly say you've spent time with Havoc and Jordan's kids and still feel that way?"

She laughed a little. "Yep. I may not be able to handle them, but Havoc doesn't seem to have any trouble, even if I have seen Jordan run away a few times. It's funny watching her hide from them."

"Before all this happened, did you have hopes or dreams for your future? Ones that don't include Officer Dipshit?"

She nodded. "I'd thought about going to college. I didn't know how it would work. There was no way my dad would let me leave and go to school elsewhere, especially after what happened to Lyssa. I think the Reaper girls will be lucky if they're ever let out of their fathers' line of sight. And now with me and Ty…"

"Why did you fall for him?" I asked. It had been weighing on me for a while. She'd grown up around bikers, and she'd been claimed by one. So why had she gone after a cop of all guys?

"He made me feel special. He listened when I talked, and the way he smiled at me made it seem like we were the only two people in the world. When he said he loved me and wanted to marry me, I thought it was a fairytale coming true." She sighed. "I should have known better. Girls like me don't end up with guys like that. Of course, he ended up being the villain in the story anyways and definitely *not* Prince Charming."

"Girls like you?" I asked.

"You know. A biker's daughter? The kids at school always looked at us different. We were the kids of outlaws. I always read books where the high school had cliques like jocks, nerds, band geeks… but not once did any of them have a group of outcasts because their dads belonged to a motorcycle club. People in town whisper about the illegal things our parents have done."

"But you had friends outside the club?"

She nodded. "A few. Some of the kids didn't care what other people said. But the super popular ones? They tried to make our lives hell. Little did they realize compared to disappointing Torch, Bull, Tank, Flicker, or even my dad, they appeared more like pissed-off fluffy bunnies."

I coughed to cover a laugh. I could imagine their expressions if she'd called them that to their faces. I'd known kids like those. Hell, every generation had the cool kids who bullied the losers and outcasts. And every damn time someone stood up to them, it only showed how weak they truly were.

"You know they were jealous of you, right? How could they not be? You were this cool girl whose dad rode a Harley. I bet their parents were paper pushers who played golf on the weekends."

I felt her smile against me as she pressed her face to me. "I remember this one time Torch decided to see what all the fuss was about. He bought some golf clubs and balls. My dad even joined in. The first time that ball didn't go where he wanted it to, he started cussing and threw the club into the woods. It's probably still there."

"I have a seriously hard time picturing Torch playing golf."

"It was quite a sight. Almost as funny as my dad giving it a go. Needless to say, they decided golf was for pussies."

I thought about it a moment. "I don't know. It's clearly a sport since they have professional tournaments. I think there's a level of skill involved, but playing just for the sake of playing? That I don't understand. I guess it's fun for some people. Maybe it's their stress reliever."

"What's yours?" she asked.

Uh. Fuck me. I couldn't very well tell her I'd banged the nearest club whore when I wanted to take the edge off. Of course, I hadn't done that since I'd agreed to make her mine. "These days, I work on my bike or help Colorado with whatever car he's rebuilding. Sometimes I stop by Doolittle's place and pet the various animals he keeps."

She sat up. "Animals? What kinds?"

Was it too late to recall those words? Why did I get the sudden feeling my house was about to be invaded by things with fur, feathers, and scales? Shit. All the women oohed and aahed over Doolittle and his little zoo.

"Um. All sorts, I guess. Depends on what he's rescued lately. He has a clinic in town, but he tends to pick up strays or take in animals people can't keep, or shouldn't have had to begin with. At one point, there was a tiger here."

Her jaw dropped. "Tiger?"

"Yep. Doolittle put a huge cage out away from the homes and put wire across the top too so it couldn't leap or climb out. It only stayed here about a week while he found a zoo willing to take it."

She poked me in the ribs. "Can we go see his animals?"

I eyed her breasts and let my gaze skim over her curves. "Should I be offended we're lying in bed, with you completely naked, and you want to put on clothes and go pet furry creatures?"

She tipped her head to the side. "Yes. You should definitely be offended, but sorry. Bunnies, kittens, and other cutesy things sound more interesting at the moment. Besides, I got myself off in the shower. I'm good for now."

I growled and toppled her to the bed, caging her in as I settled over her. "You little hellion."

Mariah grinned up at me. "You're the one who brought up the animals. You only have yourself to blame."

Shit. She wasn't exactly wrong. I pressed my dick against her, watching as her eyes went wide and her cheeks flushed. Good. It seemed my distance hadn't killed the attraction she'd felt for me. Long as I knew she desired me, we could put sex on hold until later.

"I'll take you to pet all the critters you want, with one condition."

"What?" she asked.

I winked. "You pet *me* later."

She giggled and squirmed under me. "Deal. But just so you know, I may want you to return the favor. A girl has needs after all."

I had a feeling Mariah was going to be a handful. Maybe not quite as bad as her sister, but close. I smiled, relishing the thought of taming her. The future suddenly seemed rather bright.

Chapter Five

Mariah

When Savage had said Doolittle kept a small zoo at his house, I hadn't realized how literal he was being. Doolittle's house was off on its own, and for good reason. He had a pen for small livestock, another where a donkey grazed, another with what appeared to be two llamas, a chicken coop, several dog runs, and an aviary. He'd even put out a kiddie pool of water and had three ducklings paddling around in it.

"I didn't believe you," I said. "I thought he'd have a few cats and dogs. But this…"

"A little overwhelming, but he has a permit to rehab pretty much any animal he wants. Not to mention the medical training to back it up. He may treat domestic animals in town, but he also has a background in treating wildlife of various sorts."

"Wow." I looked around with wide eyes while we waited on the man to open the door. What if he wasn't home? Could I at least get a closer look at everything outside? My fingers itched to pet something.

The door opened and the man standing on the other side had a small monkey on his shoulder and a baby sling strapped to his chest that clearly had something inside it. My mouth opened and shut as the monkey chittered and leapt from Doolittle's shoulder to mine. At least, I assumed he was Doolittle. I'd met him once, a while back, but I hadn't paid him much attention at the time.

"Looks like Reba likes you," he said, a smile curving his lips. "Hey, Savage, I think your woman needs --"

"Nope," Savage said, cutting him off. "You're not

sending a monkey home with me."

Doolittle's eyebrows arched. "Interesting. You said not a monkey, but you didn't say you would take *anything* home. I think she's already had a positive effect on you, now that you've pulled your head out of your ass."

I turned my head and coughed away from the monkey as I tried damn hard not to laugh. It seemed he'd noticed the way Savage avoided me. Glad to know it hadn't been just me. Farrah had been too preoccupied to really bother, even though she'd listened to me gripe.

Doolittle snapped his fingers and Reba leapt back onto his shoulder, chittering at him. He reached up to stroke her fur and she settled. I tried to peer into the sling, and when he noticed, he pulled the fabric back a little. I gasped at what I saw inside.

"Is that a…"

He nodded. "Yep. Baby kangaroo. And no, you can't have this one. I've already called the wildlife places, and one of them is making arrangements to come get him. Someone decided he'd make a great pet, except it's illegal to have him in this state. Same with Reba. I have a special permit that allows me to rehab animals, even those not allowed as pets in the state. So Reba is fine for now, but eventually I'll have to find her a home either outside of the state or with a zoo or wildlife sanctuary. Same for a lot of the animals I take in."

"What else do you have?" I asked.

Doolittle stepped back. "Come on in and find out."

The front part of his home seemed normal enough, despite the five cat trees I counted. How many did he have? I hadn't seen a single animal except the two he carried with him. Dog bowls were on the floor in the kitchen, as in multiple ones, even though I didn't see any dogs either.

But as we passed the kitchen, what I assumed were bedrooms, and a hall bathroom, we went through a door that opened up into what could only be described as his own personal critter sanctuary. The glassed-in room was the same width as the house, and had to extend out thirty feet, maybe more. The tiled floor had drains in a few spots, probably to make it easier to keep the place clean.

He had several cages of birds. Some small and a few larger parrots. Another cage had several ferrets inside. He'd arranged some dividers to create a dark corner in one area, and I noticed some tanks and cages over there as well. Three bunnies hopped past, chasing each other and playing in the open floorspace.

"I don't even know where to start looking," I said.

Doolittle chuckled. "This place has that effect on people. At the moment, I have three ferrets, four guinea pigs, two chinchillas, the three rabbits you just saw racing by, an African Gray parrot, a green-cheeked conure, yellow-naped Amazon, four cockatiels, a half dozen budgies, and at least as many finches. There are also lizards, turtles, frogs. I did have a sugar glider, but she had cancer and had to be put to sleep last week."

Savage shook his head and took a step closer to the door, clearly wanting no part of the craziness going on in the room. He'd said he came here, though. He had to come out into this particular area, didn't he? Or did he visit with the cats and dogs I hadn't seen on the way through?

Doolittle nodded to the large windows. "You saw everything I have outside right now. Sometimes I get sheep or goats. I've taken in a horse or two, or brought them here for vet care since my clinic doesn't have space for them. The main area of the house currently has six kittens, three adult cats, and four dogs."

"How do you have time to take care of all these animals? No, I think what I really want to know is how can you afford to feed all of them?" I asked.

He smiled. "I get donations. Some people shove money into a jar at the clinic, because they know what I do when I'm not at work. I also have a donation button on the clinic website specifically for taking care of this crew. When someone abandons an animal, like the litter of kittens I have right now, I typically ask for either a bag of food or some other type of donation to off-set the costs. It's still cheaper than them keeping them so most people don't mind."

"What about local stores?" I asked. "Would any of the ones who carry pet food be willing to donate a bag or two a month?"

"They may. I haven't ever asked." Doolittle tipped his head to the side. "You want to come help me out once or twice a week? Meredith stops by from time to time as well, but I'll never turn down an extra set of hands."

"I'd love to." I smiled as the bunnies hopped back across the room again. "Are most of these looking for homes? The ones that aren't illegal to keep?"

He nodded. "Yeah. Any interest in adopting a new family member? The birds, rabbits, ferrets, chinchillas, most of the dogs, and all of the kittens need a home. Or are you more into lizards?"

"Don't I get a say in this?" Savage asked from behind me.

I looked over my shoulder at him. "Are you

saying I can't bring a new baby home? Something to love and care for, to spend time with me when you're not around?"

I knew it was a low blow and he winced at the reminder he'd been running from me the past year. He sighed and waved a hand at the room. I smiled and checked out all the different animals. The birds were beautiful, if a bit noisy. I couldn't really see the chinchillas since they were hiding in some sort of house inside the cage. The ferrets watched me as I stared at them, but none came to say hi. I made my way around the room before deciding none of the animals in here were right for me. I'd have loved to watch the bunnies all day, and I noticed Doolittle had them litter box trained, but I had a feeling rabbit proofing the house wouldn't be easy.

"Can I see the kittens and dogs?" I asked.

Doolittle walked out of the room and I followed. As we neared the living room, I saw two small splotches of color inside a cubby on one of the cat trees. I approached slowly and peeked inside, smiling at the little kittens curled up sleeping. Reaching inside, I stroked first one and then the other. They blinked at me, yawned widely, then tumbled out onto the platform.

"How old are these two?" I asked.

"The gray tabby is a boy and he's about twelve weeks. The white one with two different colored eyes is a girl, and my best estimate is she's fourteen weeks. I haven't neutered or spayed them yet. I usually wait until they're about five to six months old. You'd have to bring them to the clinic when it's time. I did start their vaccines, but they aren't quite done yet."

I heard Savage sigh and glanced at him. He'd narrowed his eyes on the kittens, but when our gazes met, I knew he'd let me have them both. He shook his head and gave me a slight smile.

"Can I have them?" I asked Doolittle. "Both of them?"

He grinned. "Yeah. You'll have to put them in a carrier to take them home. Keep it until you can get one. Just drop mine off on the porch when you're done with it."

"Mariah, we need to get supplies before you bring them home. We can get a kennel at the same time," Savage said. "Can't take them home with no litter boxes, food, dishes, or toys."

I poked my lower lip out as I petted the two little furballs. I wanted to take them right now, but what he said made sense. Didn't mean I had to like it. "Can we go now?"

Savage chuckled. "Yeah, we can go now. Doolittle will keep them safe for you until we have the house set up."

The gray tabby purred and rubbed his face against my hand. "You're such a little angel."

The white girl meowed at me but seemed content to wait her turn. I gave them both affection before I took Savage's hand and started dragging him to the door. Doolittle laughed as we left. I couldn't wait to bring the little kitties home. They were too cute, and so sweet.

"Good thing we didn't come over here on my motorcycle," Savage said.

"But we walked. How is that a good thing?"

"Because we can walk over to the clubhouse and use one of the trucks. I'll have to get you a car so you can get around town on your own. Should have thought of it before now."

I chewed my bottom lip. "I have one. For

whatever reason, my dad didn't send it to me. I don't even know if he kept it. He could have sold it, or maybe he's holding it for my little brother."

"Isn't he only thirteen?" he asked.

"Fourteen now, but it doesn't mean Dad won't hold onto it so Dawson can use it to learn how to drive. I haven't asked about it. I guess I figured if he wanted me to have it, he'd have sent it or brought it himself."

Savage nodded. "All right. Well, let's assume after all this time, he's not giving it to you. Do you have a preference when it comes to vehicles? Since you'd mentioned wanting kids, it definitely needs a back seat."

"What about an SUV? It would be roomy enough so you wouldn't feel cramped, and have plenty of space for the fur babies, or any human ones that come along."

"I'll get something for you by end of the week."

By the time we reached the clubhouse, I felt like I'd run a few miles. I clearly needed to get into better shape. I waited outside while Savage went into the clubhouse to get the keys to the truck. Part of me wanted to go inside, and yet, I wasn't sure I could handle seeing any club whores hang on him. I'd end up beating their asses. I didn't know the officers of the Devil's Fury well enough to pull a stunt like that right now.

I knew I should have spoken up more about how I felt. Not just with Farrah but with Savage and the others. A lot of the heartache from the last year could have been avoided if I had. Instead, I jumped at every chance to spend time with the other old ladies, especially my sister, but the few times I'd tried talk to any of the guys, I'd been shut down pretty quick. I'd wondered if they thought I was betraying Savage by talking to them. Had they thought I was flirting with them?

I shifted foot to foot, looking around. Minutes ticked by and I started to get impatient. What the hell was taking so long? I cracked my neck and went up closer to the door, standing in the shade. I could hear music pulsing inside the building, even though the sun hadn't even set. I knew my dad's club saved the parties for nighttime, but it seemed the Devil's Fury didn't abide by the same rules.

After another minute, I pushed open the door and went inside. The interior was dim, and it took my eyes a moment to adjust. As I scanned the room, my brow furrowed. I didn't see Savage anywhere. Looking over at the bar, I noticed the Prospect filling drinks kept eyeing me nervously. Was I not supposed to be here? Savage hadn't said anything about having to stay outside. I'd volunteered since he'd only been running inside to grab a set of keys.

I started across the room, bypassing the bar, and heading for the back hall. Maybe he'd gone to the office? I didn't know the layout of this place, but I knew at the Dixie Reapers, the office was the last room down the hall. I hoped the Devil's Fury would be the same way. Otherwise, I might open a door and find more than I bargained for. Last thing I wanted was to see anyone's ass as they pumped into a club whore.

The deep timbre of Savage's voice drew me to a halt outside the bathroom. Was he seriously in there having a conversation? I hesitated only a moment before shoving the door open and stepping into the room.

"Savage?" I called out.

I heard a muffled *shit* right before I rounded the corner and my jaw dropped. A beautiful blonde with tear-streaked cheeks stood in front of him, her arms wrapped around herself. What the hell?

"It's not what you think," Savage said.

"Really?" I eyed the woman, then him. "Exactly what is it you believe I'm thinking right now?"

A small rubber ball rolled across the floor from under the bathroom stall door and I frowned at it. What the absolute fuck was going on? I moved across the room, sidestepping Savage when he tried to stop me, and opened the metal door. And I stared. Hard. A little girl grinned up at me, probably no more than two or three. But it was her eyes that glued my feet to the floor.

"Savage," I said, a hint of warning in my tone. "What. The. Fuck? You forget to tell me something?"

I winced after I said the words. I knew better than to cuss in front of kids. With my luck, she'd repeat it -- a lot. Just like Farrah had when she'd been younger, or so my parents frequently said.

"It's not his fault," the blonde said softly.

"So he accidentally fell in your..." I eyed the child. "V-A-G-I-N-A and created a baby?"

"She's not mine," the woman said, wiping the tears from her face. "She's my cousin's daughter. Destiny used to come here frequently several years ago. Then one day she showed up at my family's house, pregnant, and begging for help. She refused to tell anyone here about the baby, insisting she didn't know who the father was, and that he wouldn't want her anyway."

I looked at the little girl again. "Why is she in the stall?"

"She just recently potty trained. She had to go, and I let her handle it herself," the woman said. "I tried to leave her at the gate, but the guy out there forced us to come in here. The moment Savage walked in, and I saw his eyes, I knew Camille was his."

"Camille?" I asked, eyeing the child again. I waved at the little girl and she grinned up at me. Shit. Savage had a kid? I didn't know what to make of all this. Hadn't life thrown enough crap my way already?

"Camille St. John, but I'm sure after a paternity test, it would be easy enough to get her last name changed," the woman said. "I'm Bethany. I've been trying to take care of her since Destiny ran off, thinking she'd eventually show up again. But…"

The woman folded in on herself and started sobbing. Savage awkwardly patted her back while looking uncomfortable as hell. I sighed and picked up the little girl, carrying her over to her daddy. I couldn't quite wrap my brain around the fact Savage had a kid. I'd adjusted to the fact a man had claimed me without my knowledge. But a child I hadn't known about? Then again, he hadn't been told she existed either. Had he knocked up anyone else? Would there be more surprises coming?

I thrust her into his arms and led Bethany over to the sink and helped her splash cool water on her face. I wouldn't take my frustration out on the little girl. None of this was her fault. I'd imagine she had to be rather confused. Whether I liked it or not, the fact Savage said she was his meant she was mine now too. She seemed sweet, and I had to admit she was rather adorable.

I glanced over them. She stared at Savage, her lower lip trembling. I had a feeling she'd burst into tears any moment. They were strangers still, and I hoped it wouldn't take her long to warm up to him. I could only imagine how much it would hurt to have your own kid be afraid of you.

"Destiny is dead," Savage said. "And Bethany can't take care of Camille."

"Then I guess I better let Doolittle know we're going toddler shopping instead of kitten shopping. Or maybe we can do both." I wasn't sure if Savage was up for taking on both a toddler and two kittens. It would not only be a huge change in his life, but the fur kids and human one would need a lot of attention.

"Camille would adore kittens. She loves animals," Bethany said, wiping the tears from her cheeks. "I'm sorry to just drop her here like this. I love her, I really do, but I can barely take care of myself. I suffer from depression, and it gets so bad sometimes I have to stay at a facility for anywhere from a week to a month to get it back under control. I'm not the right person to take care of her."

Camille reached for me, and I held out my hands. She launched herself at me.

"Ma, ma, ma, ma...." She buried her face in my neck and grabbed a handful of my hair, holding on tight. Her voice sounded odd to me, but I couldn't place what seemed different.

"She doesn't remember Destiny," Bethany said softly. "That's probably a good thing. She'd have been a shit mother. And I've told her I'm her aunt. It's obviously not true, but it was the easiest explanation as to who I am to her."

I rubbed Camille's back and wondered why it felt like my heart was breaking. I closed my eyes and breathed in her baby scent before coming to a decision. This little girl clearly belonged to Savage, even if he hadn't had a paternity test yet, and since I belonged to him too, that made Camille half mine. I may not have given birth to her, but it looked like I had a daughter just the same.

"All right. What things did you bring with you?" I asked Bethany.

She gave me a watery smile and blew out a breath. "Thank you. I can't even imagine how you must feel right now, and I'm so sorry for springing her on you. The way she's clinging to you tells me she'll be fine. I have a few things in the car for her, but she'll still need quite a bit. When Destiny left, she didn't have much, and Camille outgrew it all pretty quick. What little I could give her hasn't been enough. I didn't want to get child services involved."

"It's okay." My gaze locked with Savage's. "We'll make sure she has everything she needs. Right, Daddy?"

He cleared his throat, his cheeks turning a little pink as he looked away. "Right."

It looked like our relationship would be placed on the back burner again. At this rate, I'd die a virgin.

Chapter Six

Savage

Mariah was handling this far better than me. I couldn't even remember Destiny, even though Bethany had shown me a picture. Didn't matter. She was right when she said Camille had my eyes. I'd still have the paternity test done, just in case we needed proof. In the meantime, I'd ask Outlaw to hack into the state's vital records and make sure my name was on Camille's birth certificate and change her last name from St. John to Turner.

Bethany's words still tumbled in my mind. Before Mariah had found us, she'd told me about Destiny being found in a shallow grave off the side of the highway in the middle of nowhere. Dumped like unwanted trash. Her wrists and ankles had been bruised, like she'd been restrained, quite a few of her teeth had been missing, and someone had carved her up like a damn turkey. The fact she'd also been raped sent warning bells off in my head.

While it was possible she'd just pissed off the wrong person, my gut said something more was going on. I'd ask Outlaw to dig into the police reports and see if there might be more to it. The club had dealt with so much ugliness over the years. It would be nice to get a break from it all, but I wouldn't sit back while monsters roamed the earth. If I could make a difference, I would. Not just because it was the right thing to do, but also because I wanted this world to be safer for Mariah and Camille.

Bad enough Chief Daniels thought Officer Clarke might walk. Even though he'd gathered enough evidence to have the man arrested, apparently the prosecution was having trouble. They weren't sure they had a case. If that fucker came for Mariah, I'd put him six feet under.

Bethany put a car seat into the back seat of the truck, as well as a diaper bag and a small box. My daughter still clung to Mariah, and I couldn't blame her. Poor kid's world had been turned upside down more than once. First she'd been left with Bethany, and now me. Why the fuck hadn't Destiny brought her here? She had to know the club would take care of the girl. We might very well have given Destiny shit for getting knocked up, but as long as she hadn't demanded money from us it wouldn't have been an issue, no matter how suspicious some of us were.

Mariah let Bethany hug Camille one more time before putting her into the car seat. I rubbed the back of my neck, wondering how the fuck I'd gone from catching my woman getting herself off in the shower, to agreeing to adopt two kittens, to having a daughter I'd never heard about before. Could this day get any fucking weirder?

I groaned as I saw Doolittle's donkey go racing by with two llamas chasing after it. I shouldn't have even silently asked the universe that damn question. It never ended well. Bethany looked at the animals, shook her head, and got in her car without another word to either of us. She hadn't given me her number, but she knew where to find me if she decided to see Camille. I helped Mariah into the truck and took a moment to gather my courage. I wasn't sure how well I'd cope with fatherhood. Regardless, it looked like I was going to find out.

"Any other surprises I should prepare for?" Mariah asked as I got into the truck.

"Fuck, I hope not. I'm getting too old for this shit."

Mariah snickered and reached over to pat my thigh, which only made my dick remember she'd been naked and pressed against me not that long ago. Great. Now I'd be buying toddler shit while walking around with a hard cock. I pinched the bridge of my nose.

"I have no idea what she needs," I said.

"I'd text my mom, but she hasn't had a kid that small in a while. But I can ask Pepper, Katya, and Delphine. They each have a toddler. I'd ask Farrah, but... I thought you might want to talk to your club first. The moment I tell Farrah you have a daughter, everyone will know. They may anyways, since everyone saw us walk out of there with Camille."

I nodded. "Start with the Dixie Reapers' ladies. Just be prepared. They'll ask why you need to know, then they'll go running to your mom with the news I have a kid no one knew about, and it's just going to spiral from there. Not telling Farrah now will only slow the gossip down a bit."

"It's okay. I'm used to it."

She started tapping at her phone screen and I decided to go to a strip mall that had stores for a little bit of everything. I remembered Elena talking about the kids' shop she'd found there that carried both new and consignment items. Seemed like a good spot to start. The same set of stores also had a pet shop, so we could get the supplies we'd need for the kittens.

So much for the plans I'd had for Mariah tonight. Looked like we'd be putting things on hold for another day or so while everyone adjusted. I didn't know a damn thing about my daughter, other than her name and that her mom had been a club whore who'd died violently.

"Can you reach the box in back?" I asked. "I wonder if there's any paperwork in there."

Mariah turned, getting on her knees and putting her ass in the air to reach into the back floorboard. She turned around with a folder in her hand. "Well, good news number one, this looks like it has important papers in it. Good news number two, Camille is asleep. Looks like car rides knock her out, or the stress from today did it."

"What's in the file?" I asked.

She pawed through the papers, her brow furrowed, her lip caught between her teeth. "Birth certificate. Shot records. More medical stu... ff. Shit."

"What?" I glanced at her and noticed she looked a little green.

"Um. According to the information in this folder, she can't hear. I don't understand. She called me momma. I'd thought maybe she'd been listening to what everyone was saying. Maybe she hadn't."

"Does it explain why?" I asked.

"Looks like she had some sort of infection shortly after she was born. The antibiotics they gave her caused hearing loss. I wonder if maybe she's not entirely deaf? Would it be possible for her to have regained at least part of her hearing?" Mariah asked.

"No idea, baby girl. I'll find out who the old ladies use for a pediatrician, and we'll get her in soon as we can. Does it say when her birthday is?"

She scanned the documents again. "June sixth. She's just a little over two years old, Savage."

Her phone started going off with messages and I let her look through them. If Destiny weren't dead, I might very well have strangled her. She'd kept my daughter from me for two years! From the little Bethany had given us, I had to wonder just how much Camille had missed out on so far. Had she had enough to eat? Warm enough clothes in the winter? Had she gone to a preschool?

"We need to let the rest of the club know. A few saw us walk out with Camille, but I didn't exactly stop to talk to anyone. I know the Prospects at the gate and bar would have some clue. They listen even when we don't realize it."

She wagged her phone at me. "Want me to text Farrah and have her talk to Demon? It pretty much negates me not asking her for advice, but… it's your call."

I pulled my phone from my pocket and tossed it to her. She fumbled hers trying to catch mine. The glare she gave me was cute as hell and made me smile. So ferocious!

"Zero, Six, One, Four." I hoped like fuck she wouldn't ask if the numbers meant anything.

She keyed in the code and unlocked my phone, looking at me expectantly.

"Pull up Badger's number and hit call, then put it on speaker for me. I guess if we get a family vehicle, I can sync the phones to it so this will be easier in the future."

She did as I asked and held the phone up while it rang.

"Hello," Badger answered, sounding tired as hell.

"Hey, Pres. Wanted to tell you something before you hear it elsewhere. You remember a club whore named Destiny several years back?"

He snorted. "No. I haven't been with one of those bitches since before I went to prison."

"I knocked her up. Her sister just dropped my daughter off at the clubhouse," I said, giving him a moment to absorb the words. "Her name is Camille and she's two. She's with me and Mariah right now.

Going shopping for shit she'll need so we can set up a room for her."

"You have one cleared out?" he asked.

Well, fuck me sideways. "No."

He snorted. "I'll have someone take care of it. Demon still have a key to your place?"

"Same as he does for everyone's," I said.

"All right. We'll make a spot for her. I'll order a toddler bed and dresser from the place we used to buy Ivory's stuff. Tal can run pick it up and take it to your place so it's ready when you get back."

"What about decorations?" Mariah asked.

"Something you forgot to say, Savage?" Badger asked.

"Sorry, Pres. I'm driving so I had Mariah put the call on speaker. Should have said something."

He sighed. "It's fine. I'm sure your head is spinning right now, having a kid dropped at your feet out of the blue. What kind of decorations, Mariah?"

"Her aunt said she liked animals. Maybe find a few of those wall stickers to put up? Kittens, puppies, bunnies. That sort of thing," Mariah said.

My eyebrows rose at how good she was at this mommy shit. Good thing at least one of us didn't seem quite so lost right now. I could only imagine how badly I'd fuck the kid up on my own. Having Mariah by my side through this helped keep me marginally calm.

"I'll see what I can find. That same store might have something. Want bedding with animals too?" Badger asked.

"Yes, if they have it," she said.

"I'll pay you back, Pres. Just let me know the total," I said.

"Nope. Consider it a gift. Welcome to fatherhood, Savage. Your life just got turned inside out.

But it's one hell of a ride." Badger chuckled. "I'll go get all this in motion. Any other requests before I hang up?"

"Curtains," Mariah blurted out. "Matching curtains please. And maybe a bookshelf and toybox?"

"All right. You two be careful out there."

Badger hung up before either of us could say anything else. Mariah placed my phone in the cup holder and leaned back in her seat. By the time we arrived at the strip mall, Camilla had drooled all over her shirt, but the kid was still completely out. Mariah lifted her from the car seat and held her against her chest as we went into the first shop.

"Stroller," I muttered as I grabbed a shopping cart. "We need one immediately."

"I'm fine carrying her."

"The longer you hold her, the heavier she'll feel. Trust me. When Dagger and Guardian first claimed Zoe, they made sure Luis got to know all of us. I held him once for a half hour. The first few minutes weren't bad. By the time I'd handed him off to someone else, it felt like my arms would fall off."

She snickered as we looked over the selection of strollers. Mariah hooked her foot under one with a padded seat and pulled it out, then placed Camille into the stroller and buckled her in. I noticed it had a tray with a cup holder for my daughter, and another cup holder on the handle for whichever adult was pushing her. I didn't even stop to look at the price tag. Clearly, we were buying it.

Mariah checked the sizes on Camille's clothes, thankfully without waking her, and selected a dozen shirts and pants, a few dresses, and five pair of pajamas. I felt awkward as fuck when she started flipping through the packages of panties, finally selecting some with kittens on them, then hesitating a moment before grabbing a package with rainbows and butterflies too. I noticed she also put a package of pull-ups into the cart.

"Bethany said she'd been potty training her, but I don't know how often she still has accidents," Mariah said. "Better to be prepared than having to wash clothes every day. Or sheets, for that matter."

I shot off a quick text to Badger. *Get a waterproof mattress cover too.*

It only took him a minute to respond. *Not my first time buying for a kid. Already bought two.*

Well, that certainly put me in my place. I trailed behind Mariah as she gathered shoes, socks, and stopped to check out the small selection of toys. I hadn't bothered to look in the box Bethany had packed, but something told me there weren't a lot of clothes and toys in there. It had felt too light to contain very many things, and the woman had admitted to not being able to afford much.

It sickened me to think of all the things I'd spent money on the past two years, and how my daughter had suffered, all because I hadn't known about her. Whatever it took, I'd see she had everything she needed from this point forward. I'd make sure birthdays and Christmases would become some of her happiest memories. As much as I knew it was wrong to hope she never remembered Destiny, and never asked about her, I wondered how Mariah would feel if Camille believed she was her mom.

"We need a toy store. And a bookstore," Mariah said. "This isn't going to cut it."

"What was in the box?" I asked.

"Maybe three outfits, one pair of pajamas, the paperwork, and a cloth doll that looks like it went through World War I. It might have even been around that long." She glanced at me before eyeing the meager toy offerings again. "I'm not sure she's ever had toys, Savage. Other than that doll."

Now I understood why she'd asked for a toybox. She planned to fill it so Camille would not only have plenty to do, but hopefully feel special.

"There's another shop we can stop by on the way home. Right now, let's pay for all this stuff, load it into the truck, and go get the kitten things you need," I said.

"All right." She pushed the stroller up to the register, pausing long enough to toss two cups with weird-looking lids into the cart and two sets of dishes with tiny utensils. I followed with the cart as she set off again for the front of the store. She pulled the tag from the stroller and placed it on the counter while I started to unload everything else for the woman to ring up.

The total would have made a lesser man cry. Who the hell knew kids cost so much? And I had a feeling we were only getting started. These were just the basics Camille would need. Having arrived with so little, we were having to pretty much start from ground zero. I pulled out my phone to text Badger again.

Better get multiple sheets and blankets. Mariah doesn't seem certain Camille won't wet the bed.

I got an emoji back with a man covering his face with his hand. Frowning at the phone, I wanted to text back and ask if Badger felt okay. He never used emojis. Then I realized Adalia must have responded. Either she'd hijacked his phone, or he'd given it to her.

We loaded everything into the truck, except the stroller and Camille. When I reached for her, Mariah swatted my hands away.

"The shop is just down the sidewalk, right?" she asked.

"Yeah. Last store in this strip. Why?"

"I'll walk down there with her. If you want to park closer that's fine, but no sense moving her out of the stroller just to put her right back in it."

I nodded and kissed her cheek before getting into the truck. She gave me a bemused smile as she turned to walk down the sidewalk. By the time I'd parked again and made it into the store, Mariah had already managed to pull a shopping cart and push the stroller at the same time, and the cart contained two litter boxes, a scoop, a large jug of litter, at least a dozen toys, and she looked to be seconds away from loading a cat tree into it as well.

"It didn't take me *that* damn long to park," I muttered as I grabbed the cat tree before she could and carried it under my arm.

"I want two," she said, pointing to a slightly smaller one a few spots down. I grabbed it too and followed her to the area with the food.

She put some sort of water thing with a jug on it into the cart, as well as two small bowls, then started scrolling on her phone.

"What are you doing now?" I asked.

"Searching for the top three recommended kitten foods."

I lifted my eyebrows. "Take my phone from my pocket and just text or call Doolittle. He can tell you what they've been eating, and what he'd recommend. He's going to be their vet anyway."

She smirked as she shoved her hand into my pocket, and I nearly groaned as her fingers got incredibly close to touching my dick. While she talked to Doolittle, I set the cat trees down next to the cart and took a moment to watch my daughter. Her lips moved in her sleep, like she was sucking on something, but otherwise she seemed peaceful. I wished I knew more about her. What did she like to do? What were her favorite foods?

Food. *Shit.* I needed to figure out what she ate and stock the kitchen. Did toddlers eat the same food as us?

Mariah ended the call and pointed to a large bag of kitten food on the top shelf. "Doolittle said to give them that."

I added it to the cart and lifted the cat trees again as Mariah put the phone back into my pocket. "We need to get all this stuff home and then head out again."

"Why?" she asked.

"I need to make sure the kitchen is stocked with things for Camille, and you said you wanted to go toy shopping. I'm going to have to put the cat trees and litter into the bed of the truck. Can't exactly go into stores with them sitting out in the open like that. Better to unload and then go out again. You and Camille can stay in the truck. I'll just drop everything in the front entry for now."

She nodded. "All right. Let's pay for everything and get out of here before I'm tempted to buy more stuff. Or take home another pet."

With those words, I nearly sprinted to the register. A toddler and two kittens in one day were more than enough. If she brought home anything else, I might seriously consider curling into a ball and crying like a little bitch. I still felt like I was on overload from finding out about Camille.

When life fucked with you, it did it in a big way.

Chapter Seven

Mariah

Camille had woken up while we were at the grocery store. I'd expected her to cry, want to explore, or do something other than sit calmly. So far, that's all she'd done. Even now that we were home, I could see her taking everything in, but she didn't act like other two-year-olds I'd been around. I wondered if we'd see more of a reaction when the kittens arrived. Doolittle had promised to drop them off in the morning, claiming we had enough to handle tonight with it being Camille's first night with us.

The guys had yanked everything from the room I'd been using, moved my things into Savage's bedroom, and turned the guest room into a nursery. I couldn't even grumble about it, since I'd been naked in bed with him earlier. Not to mention she needed the room far more than I did. It was beyond ridiculous I'd belonged to Savage for a year now and we'd never slept in the same room. I doubted we'd do more than sleep tonight, but it was at least a step in the right direction.

I'd washed all the bedding and made up the toddler bed for Camille, then washed her clothes. After doing a bit of research on what she should eat or drink, when she should go to bed, and what to expect in general, I felt a little more prepared, if slightly overwhelmed. If my mother knew I was now a stepmom, she hadn't called me about it. Or texted. I'd half-expected my dad to arrive on our doorstep by dinner, but he'd been quiet too.

Camille ignored the doll next to her on the floor, the one Bethany had packed. She stared at the purple teddy bear in front of her, and the set of blocks, like they were foreign objects. I'd assured her three times they were hers and she could touch them. Didn't seem to matter. Either she was too scared to reach for them, she hadn't heard me at all -- which could be possible if she really couldn't hear -- or she felt just as out of her element as we were right now. It had to be scary for her, coming to a new place, living with strangers.

I stepped out of the room long enough to yell out to Savage.

"Savage, can you come here?" I heard the tread of his boots and he appeared in the doorway a moment later. "I need to go finish up her laundry. Can you watch her for a minute? I didn't think to get a baby gate, and I don't want to close her in the room."

He nodded. "I'll call one of the Prospects and ask them to get one. Anything else we forgot?"

I looked around the room, eyeing the outlets. "We need to babyproof the entire house. Outlet covers, cabinet and drawer locks, something to make sure she can't open the doors and leave without us knowing. Basically, if it's in the baby proofing area, we need it."

"On it." He pulled out his phone and leaned against the wall while he made his call.

I rushed to the laundry room to fold the items I'd already dried, and then dry the stuff still in the washer. I'd cleaned all the lighter-colored things first, then done a load of darks. Next I'd wash the pinks and purples. I didn't want to chance anything bleeding and ruining her new clothes.

After I folded everything, I carried it to her room and placed the things in her dresser. Except one pair of pajamas, and I got out a pull-up from the new package. Even though Bethany said Camille had been potty trained, I didn't want to chance her wetting the bed the first few nights. From what I'd researched in the car on my phone, stressful situations, like being dropped off with strangers, could make her regress a little. Wetting the bed wouldn't be out of the question.

"Come on, sweetheart. Let's take bath," I said, scooping her up. I snagged the pajamas and pull-up off the top of the dresser as I walked to the hall bathroom. I'd already set out her bath stuff in here, even though her baby towels and washcloths hadn't been cleaned yet. I knew Savage had a few super soft towels that would work for tonight.

I filled the tub, added a bit of her baby soap to make some bubbles, then started to strip Camille from her clothes. By the time the water was waist-deep on her, I shut it off and gave her a few bath toys, then waited to see what she'd do. The little girl looked around the room, eyed the toys a moment, then sat perfectly still. It was... unnatural, and completely unsettling to see a toddler so calm.

I nudged the purple rubber duck, sending it across the water. Her eyes tracked the movement, but she didn't reach for it. I'd known we'd need to take her a pediatrician to have them make sure she was healthy, but I was starting to wonder if she'd need counseling. Did they offer such a thing for kids her age? Something felt very wrong. I'd never met a toddler who acted like Camille. While it was possible she was a quiet kid in general, I had a feeling something else was going on.

Savage cleared his throat behind me. "Everything all right?"

"I'm worried," I murmured.

He hunkered down behind me. "Why?"

"She's not acting like a normal toddler. It could be shock. She's had a major change in her life. More than one."

"You think it's something else, though, don't

you?" he asked.

I nodded. "What do you know about Bethany? She said she'd brought Camille here because she suffered from depression and couldn't take care of her. You don't think Camille's been abused or neglected, do you?"

"I hope the fuck not," he said, a soft growl to his voice.

I put some baby soap in my hands and rubbed them together before reaching for Camille. I washed her arms, her back, her chest and stomach. Tears burned my eyes and bile rose in my throat. The longer I touched her, the stiffer she became. Someone had hurt this sweet girl. I didn't have a doubt in my mind about it. When I helped her stand so I could wash below her waist, I saw the change immediately.

"Savage," I said softly, my heart breaking. I couldn't hold my tears back another moment.

He reached for his daughter, and she couldn't control her bladder. A keening sound escaped her as she stumbled back a step, only to freeze when he put his hands on her arms to lift her from the tub. She didn't struggle or fight. I saw the fury in his eyes as he dried her and wrapped the towel around her.

"I think I know why Bethany took off so fast," I said.

"She didn't give me any contact information. I don't even know where she lives." He took a deep breath, cradling Camille to his chest. "But I'll have every hacker we know track her down. If she had anything to do with Camille being hurt, I will end that bitch myself."

"Get in line," I muttered.

A horrible thought came to me and I pushed past Savage and went to Camille's room. I grabbed the doll off the floor and carried it to the kitchen, throwing it straight into the trash. The only reason she wouldn't have clung to a familiar toy was if it held bad memories. My stomach churned as I considered why she hadn't picked up any of her new toys either. Had they used them against her or as some sort of sick reward?

I bolted for the trashcan and threw up. Tears streaked my cheeks and I sobbed between bouts of purging my stomach. How could someone so evil exist? Why would anyone hurt an innocent child? What Ty had planned for me was bad enough. Imagining some sick bastard getting his hands on Camille made me want to burn everything to the ground.

I sank to the floor, leaning against the wall, as I cried. Savage found me a few minutes later. His arms were empty so he must have put Camille into her room. I swiped at my cheeks. "Sorry," I said, my throat feeling scratchy.

"Don't be." He sat on the floor and pulled me into his arms. I curled up in his lap, clinging to him. "I dressed her and put her to bed. She looked confused when I turned out the lights and left. Badger or Adalia bought her a nightlight. I switched it on so she wouldn't be in the dark."

"That poor baby. I can't... I..." I broke again, crying so hard I could barely breathe.

Savage ran his hand up and down my back. I felt the tension and anger in his body, and knew he wanted to kill someone for having touched his daughter. I couldn't blame him. In fact, when he found out who had done it, I wanted to help him destroy the motherfucker.

"I have never seen anyone react as strongly as

you did just now," he said. "Not when it comes to a girl you didn't give birth to. I'd thought you'd hate me when I found out I had a daughter. It didn't occur to me you'd fall in love with her right away."

I pulled back slightly and looked up into his face. "She's mine, Savage. I don't care if you have a paternity test done and it says she's not your biological daughter. From the moment Bethany left her with us, Camille became ours. Anyone ever tells me that's not my daughter, I will gut them where they stand."

He cupped my cheek. "Where's all this coming from, baby girl? Don't get me wrong. You've been great with her today. That's just a lot of emotion for a girl you didn't know existed until today. One I had with a club whore no less."

I swallowed hard at the reminder he'd knocked up one of the girls at the clubhouse. I'd grown up hearing about those women, even my mother didn't think I knew what was going on. As I'd gotten older, I'd even met a few. My dad had never found out or he'd have lost it. Most had been catty and I'd hated them on sight. Especially when the boys I'd considered my friends and extended family started to eye those same women.

But I couldn't hold all that against Camille. She hadn't chosen her mother. Knowing she could possibly be deaf, and that someone had terrified her, ripped me apart. I couldn't have hated her if I'd tried. It wasn't her fault her dad had knocked up a club whore. The moment Savage said she was his daughter, she'd become mine too. I had no fucking idea what I was doing. I'd never been one to babysit the younger kids at the club. Now I was wishing I had.

He stared at me intently and I realized I hadn't answered his question yet. How did I explain something I didn't quite understand myself? "She's been hurt. Probably has felt alone. My heart is breaking for her. I will do whatever it takes to make her feel safe. I know you and my dad said Ty planned to sell me. But I could have endured it. That little girl in there doesn't have a single way to defend herself against the monsters in the world. She doesn't understand why anyone would hurt her, especially in such an awful way."

"Easy, baby. We don't know for certain what happened. It's obvious someone hurt her, and my suspicions are the same as yours, but we're just guessing right now." He tucked my hair behind my ear. "We'll do whatever we can to find out what happened to her. And I promise those fuckers will pay, even if it's Bethany or another woman. Evil is evil. Doesn't matter what gender they are."

"What do we do now?" I asked.

"Well, I'm going to carry you to our room and start the shower. I think the hot water would do you good right about now. Then we'll go to sleep and start fresh tomorrow. We can call a doctor and set up an appointment and go from there."

"All right." I snuggled into him again. "I feel overwhelmed, and then I realized Camille must be so lost. She hasn't ever met us before and now she's living here. And if she can't hear, then she understands even less."

Savage ran his hand up and down my back again in long, soothing strokes. "One day at a time, baby girl."

"Right. I can do that." I blew out a breath. I only hoped I hadn't just lied to the both of us. I felt like I'd gotten off an amusement park ride and everything was still spinning. This morning I'd thought Savage didn't want anything to do with me. Then I'd found out he did want me, and I'd thought we'd be having sex for the first time. Instead, we'd discovered he had a daughter and our world had exploded.

I should be used to it, all the ups and down. Even if my dad had tried to shield his daughters from the ugliness the club dealt with, I'd heard enough over the years to understand how awful the world could be. None of this was new, except this time it affected me and my family. Finding out Ty hadn't really loved me and had only used me had been painful, and left me feeling out of sorts, but this... this was different. "When you find whoever hurt her, don't you dare take them out," I said.

His hand stopped moving. "I'm not going to let that monster keep breathing."

"You misunderstand. I know you'll want to protect not only her, but me too. I don't want you to. I want to face whoever hurt her, tell them exactly what I think of them, and I want to make them bleed."

Savage cupped my chin and lifted my face to meet his gaze. "Bloodthirsty little thing, aren't you?"

"I will die to protect our family, Savage. Never doubt it. I'm not just some dainty woman to keep in your house. I'm the daughter of a Dixie Reaper and I was born to this way of life. I'm not afraid to get my hands dirty."

He smiled softly, then pressed his lips to mine in a quick, hard kiss. "You're fucking perfect, Mariah. I couldn't have chosen a better old lady if I'd tried."

"Let's go to bed. I'm over this day."

He nodded and stood, lifting me into his arms. Savage carried me off to the bedroom and as promised, he started the shower. I didn't bother shutting the door or pretending to be modest. He'd already seen me naked. Felt my breasts pressed up against him. Besides, I was his and he was mine. I didn't see the point in trying to hide from him.

* * *

Savage

I heard the water shut off in the shower and set my phone aside. I'd sent a message to Outlaw with what little I knew about Camille, Destiny, and Bethany. He knew exactly what I wanted him to find, and what I worried had happened. On the plus side, he'd given me the name of his kids' pediatrician and even offered to set up an appointment. The doctor saw all the club's kids, so it wasn't unusual for someone other than the parent to set something up. We helped each other when and where we could.

Mariah stepped into the bedroom, rubbing a towel through her hair. And I pushed myself upright. What. The. Fuck. I couldn't stop staring as the goddess I got to call mine approached the bed wearing not a single damn thing. She hadn't even wrapped her towel around her body. Nope. She just used it to wring the moisture from her hair as she walked toward me naked, as if she'd done it a million times before.

My cock certainly appreciated her boldness. It already tented the sheet.

"Not that I'm going to complain about the excellent view, but… what are you doing?" I asked.

She arched her eyebrows. "It's not like you've never held me. Or seen me naked for that matter."

"Except things are a little different this time. You aren't all excited about going to see animals, and we have the entire night. Providing Camille stays asleep."

A smile curved her lips as she tossed the towel into the bathroom and slid into bed next to me. She propped her head on her hand as she reached out to tug the sheet lower. I nearly grabbed it but decided to see just how far she'd go. It hadn't been but twenty minutes since I'd found her sobbing in the kitchen. Her eyes were still puffy and a little red-rimmed. I hadn't thought she'd want to start that part of our lives tonight.

"Mariah, we don't have to do anything tonight. The moment I saw Camille I knew our plans had changed. Hell, I didn't even know if you'd want to stay with me at all. It wouldn't have surprised me if you'd packed up and moved out, and I sure the fuck wouldn't have blamed you. You didn't sign on for this."

She reached up to run her fingers along the whiskers on my jaw. "Technically, I didn't sign up for any of it. My dad's club volunteered me. I'm not a quitter, Savage. You may have claimed me without my knowledge, but if I didn't walk out of here anytime in the last year, I'm damn sure not going to do it now. You need me. *She* needs me. And maybe I need the both of you too."

Mariah sat up on her knees and yanked the sheet off me. My cock twitched at the thought of her soft fingers stroking me. She ran a fingertip along the length of my dick, her nail lightly scraping the head. I sucked in a breath and put my hands behind my head. Otherwise, I'd grab her, throw her on the bed, and be balls-deep inside her in less than ten seconds.

"You want to play?" I asked.

She licked her lips and nodded.

"All right. There are rules." Her gaze locked on mine. "Rule number one. I'm in charge. Whether we're in the bedroom or outside the house, I'm always in charge. Unless I tell you otherwise. And tonight, I'm damn sure in charge."

Her breath caught and she gave me a little nod. Her pulse fluttered in her throat and I realized it didn't bother her at all to give up control to me. I wondered how far I could push her. No, what I really wanted to know was whether or not that asshole cop had bossed her around in the bedroom. I didn't want her comparing the two of us.

"Second rule, if you want me to stop because something I've told you to do is either painful or a very hard limit for you, then we need a safe word."

"Safe word? Did we just fall into a movie?" She looked around the room. "This doesn't look like a dungeon."

Fuck me. "What the hell do you know about dungeons?"

She shrugged a shoulder as if it weren't important. "Enough. Am I supposed to call you Master? Or Sir?"

"No, but when you disobey, you'll be punished. Understood?"

She nodded. "My safe word is... feathers."

"Feathers?" I asked, making certain I'd heard her right.

"Yep. Feathers."

I wondered if there was some meaning behind her choice. I wasn't about to ask right now, but maybe later. If I remembered. It had been so long since I'd been inside a woman, I wasn't sure I wouldn't blow immediately. I'd be embarrassed as fuck if I did that, and have to make it up to her.

I spread my legs a little and jerked my chin in that direction. "Kneel right there. I want a good view of you sucking my cock."

Her nipples went rock hard at my words and I

knew we were about to have a rather memorable first night as a true couple. She hurried to obey, pulling her hair over one shoulder. Mariah leaned down and her breath fanned over the head of my cock before she flicked her tongue out to taste the pre-cum beading there. She opened her mouth, ready to swallow me whole, and I stopped her.

"No." She froze and waited. "Lick the head and down the shaft. Don't put me all the way in your mouth yet."

Her tongue dragged across the head before she gave short, quick flicks down the shaft and back up. *Holy shit!* I felt my balls draw up and I held my breath, hoping like fuck I wasn't about to come already. I watched as she teased me, and noticed she'd started to squirm a bit. Seemed like my girl enjoyed what she was doing.

"Suck me," I commanded.

Her lips closed over my cock and slid down until I bumped the back of her throat. I groaned at how incredible it felt. She sucked hard, her cheeks hollowing when she pulled back, only to swallow me down again. I knew I wouldn't last much longer. Reaching down, I gripped her hair in my hand and controlled her motion. On the next stroke, I held her still, my cock at the back of her throat. I saw her eyes widen and knew she was about to panic so I let her go and she came up for air.

"Good girl." I eyed the perfection of her body. "There are so many things I want to do to you, but I can't do them all at once. I want to see your tits bounce while you ride me. I want to fuck you from behind. I want you to slide your ass down my cock and ride me while I play with your pussy."

"Savage." My name was nearly a whimper on

her lips.

"Gates. Call me Gates, baby. When we're in the bedroom at any rate." I crooked a finger at her, and she crawled up my body until she straddled my abdomen. I reached up and cupped her breasts, rubbing my thumbs across her nipples. She shivered, her eyes going dark with need. I gave the hard tips a little pinch and tug, and I felt the moisture slip from her pussy. "Seems my baby likes her bedroom activities to have a little bite to them. Did you like that slight sting of pain?"

She nodded.

"You trust me?" I asked.

"Yes. I trust you, Gates."

I reached into the bedside table drawer and pulled out a length of soft rope. I'd tossed it in there after the first time I'd yanked one out to thoughts of Mariah, hoping one day I'd get to use it on her.

"Hands behind your back." She crossed her wrists at her lower back and I looped the rope around them, securing her just tight enough she couldn't escape but not enough to hurt her. "I'm going to play with your pretty pussy and your gorgeous tits until you come and beg me to fuck you. Then I'll bend you over the bed and take what I want."

She stared at me, not uttering her safe word, just watching and waiting. It seemed I hadn't gone too far yet. I had to remind myself she'd been with that fucking cop. It wasn't like she'd never been touched.

"Lean back. Show me your pussy."

She shifted her weight so she could comply with my demands. The lips parted and I saw her clit poke out, already hard and slick. I spread her open more, letting my fingers graze the inside of her folds with a light touch. She moaned and wiggled her hips. I brushed her clit and she cried out.

"How badly do you need my cock, baby? Want me to fill you up? Make you mine?"

She nodded eagerly. "Please, Gates. I'm already close."

"I've barely touched you." I brushed her clit again and she shuddered, a flush tinging her cheeks. She really *was* close to coming. Damn. "Come for me, Mariah. I want you all slick and soft when I fuck you."

I worked her clit faster and harder. It didn't take much before she detonated, screaming out my name as her body stiffened and she threw her head back. Her breasts heaved as she panted and twitched with aftershocks.

I gripped her waist and lifted her. Bending her over the side of the bed, I stood behind her and kicked her feet apart. "Spread your legs."

She trembled as she tried to obey. I smiled when I realized I'd turned her legs to jelly with just one orgasm. My hand cracked down on her ass, and she yelped.

"I said to spread!"

She managed to part her thighs more and I leaned back to admire the view. I pulled her ass cheeks apart, opening her pussy even more. Without any warning, I lined my cock up and thrust into her. She tensed and screamed out, and I froze.

"Mariah?" I ran a hand down her spine. "Baby, did I hurt you?"

"I… I haven't…" She cleared her throat and turned to look at me. I noticed moisture in her eyes and felt like shit. Had I made her cry? "You're my first."

My heart slammed against my ribs and a buzzing filled my ears. "What?"

"I haven't had a cock inside me until just now. It

hurt for a minute, but I'm okay now. If you want to move."

Oh, I moved all right. I leaned down over her back, putting our faces closer together. "What the fuck do you mean you've never had a cock in your pussy before? When I told you I hadn't touched anyone since claiming you, you said you'd been with that dickhead cop."

She shook her head. "We only fooled around, and…"

"And what?" I asked, a slight snarl coming out of me.

"He told me how he liked his cock sucked. I got him off when we'd get together, and he'd touch me, but he said he wanted to wait until we were married before going any further." She blinked. "He was grooming me, I think. Training me enough without taking my virginity. I just hadn't realized it."

I closed my eyes and pressed my forehead to her shoulder. "Jesus fucking Christ. You should have told me, baby. I'd have been gentler. I sure the hell wouldn't have tied you up."

She was quiet a moment. "I like what we're doing, Gates. Please don't stop. I promise it doesn't hurt anymore."

My cock twitched inside her, eager to keep going. I pulled my hips back and slowly pushed back in, watching to make sure she hadn't lied about the pain. When she wiggled her hips a little, I took that to mean she truly was all right. I gripped her hips and drove into her, thrusting hard and deep. I worked a hand between her and the bed so I could stroke her clit while I claimed her pussy.

She squeezed me tight when she came, and fuck if she didn't pull every drop of cum from my balls immediately. I came before I even realized it. I kept driving into her, pounding my cum deep inside her. By the time I stopped, sweat slicked our skin. I reached down and untied her wrists, massaging them lightly. I didn't want to pull free of her body. She felt so warm and tight, so fucking perfect... so... Mine!

"You okay, baby?" I asked, running my fingers through her hair.

"More than." She gave me a tired smile. "I could sleep like this, except I don't think my legs will hold me much longer."

I let my cock slip free of her body and lifted her onto the bed. While she got situated, I went into the bathroom and got a wet rag to clean her up. I saw the streaks of blood and felt both horrible for having hurt her and like a damn king for being her first. No one had been inside her except me, and since I didn't plan to ever let her go, I would be her one and only the rest of our lives.

I got into bed and pulled her into my arms. My cock hadn't softened much and poked at her ass, but there wasn't much I could do about it. Shifting a little, I trapped it between us. Not a perfect solution, but it would do for now.

"Sleep, beautiful girl." I kissed the side of her neck. "I have a feeling tomorrow will be another rough day."

She sighed and murmured something. I leaned up to get a better look at her and smiled when I realized she'd already fallen asleep. Two orgasms and she was out. I would have to remember that. If I wanted to play all night, I'd have to give her more of a break, or just keep making her come until I was done with her. I didn't think she'd complain too loudly about lots of orgasms. Most women wouldn't.

I kissed her shoulder and rubbed my chin against her soft skin. "Night, sweetheart."

I felt a warmth spread through me, a contentment I'd never experienced before. My daughter slept down the hall, and my woman lay in my arms. Didn't get much better than this.

Chapter Eight

Mariah

I glared at the doctor as Camille screamed and tried to get away from him. She'd freaked out when he'd had us strip her down to her panties. He'd listened to her heart, checked her ears, but when he'd tried to look at her throat, she'd refused. The doctor had pressed on her bottom lip, trying to get her to open, and she'd lost it.

"That's it. You're done," I told the asshole.

He backed up. "I'm not trying to distress your daughter, Ms. Turner. It's clear she's suffered a trauma. I just want to give a thorough exam, so we'll know exactly where we stand."

I wasn't going to correct him. Technically, I wasn't Ms. Turner. I might belong to Savage, but we weren't married.

"I gave you her medical records," I said.

I felt Savage's hand at my waist. He gave me a slight squeeze, and I knew he wanted me to calm down. I couldn't. Not when Camille screamed and cried. Her face had become a dark red and I worried she'd hurt herself trying to get away from everyone.

"Without further testing I can't say much about her hearing loss. She'll need to see a specialist for that. As to the other…" His gaze softened as he looked at Camille. "It's my opinion she's been abused. As much as I hate to say it, her reactions indicate sexual trauma. I can make a recommendation if you'd like. She'll need therapy, not just now, but possibly for quite a while."

I lifted Camille into my arms and held her close. She gripped my shirt in her fist and buried her face against me. I smoothed my hand over her back, hoping to calm her further. She didn't tense like she had in the bath, which meant she felt men were the bigger threat right now. I wanted to throw up again.

I picked her shirt up off the padded table and worked it over her head. It wasn't easy holding onto her and getting her dressed again, but I hoped she'd feel safer once she'd been covered. By the time I pulled her leggings up, she'd quieted and seemed content. Savage held my gaze and I knew we were both outraged and heartbroken over whatever she'd suffered. I had to wonder if not knowing was the worst part. My imagination ran wild with possibilities, each one more horrific than the first. Our world was dark and ugly sometimes, and knowing some sick, twisted person had touched Camille made me want to rage and rip everything apart.

I pressed a kiss to her forehead. "You hungry, sweetie?"

She didn't react and I just hugged her tighter. I tuned out the doctor while I gathered Camille's things and stepped out of the room. I'd let Savage handle whatever was left of the visit, but Camille and I were done. I didn't think either of us would make it in that room much longer. I walked to the front lobby, informed the receptionist Savage would take care of the bill, and I went out onto the sidewalk to wait for him.

The sunlight hit us and Camille lifted her head. She looked around and waved a hand at some birds in a nearby tree. She'd love the kittens when we got them. I'd had to ask Doolittle to hold off a bit longer since we had this appointment first thing today. I still wanted those fur babies, and I had a feeling they'd be part of the healing process for Camille. I just didn't think this morning was the best time to introduce them to their new home. Doolittle had promised to bring them by just after dinner.

Savage stepped out of the doctor's office and placed his hand on my hip. "You two okay?"

I nodded. "Just needed to get out of there, and I'm sure she did too. What did he say after I left?"

"Not much. I've got the number to a counselor who works with kids Camille's age, as well as a referral to an audiologist. The specialist couldn't get her in for another two months. We'll just have to do the best we can until then."

"I think we could all use some food and a bit of fun before heading home." I leaned against him. "If she can't hear us, I don't know how to make her understand she's safe and loved except to show her through our actions. Hugging her is hit and miss. Sometimes she seems to take comfort from it, and other times it's like she thinks something bad is coming."

He kissed the top of my head. "Let's go to the diner. It's just down the street. Maybe Camille will like a grilled cheese sandwich. Should be easy for her to eat."

"All right. Let's see how lunch goes and figure out where we're heading next. I don't know if she's ever been to the park before."

"Do we need to drive to the diner?" I asked.

"Nope. It's about one block down. If she gets heavy, I can carry her."

I eyed Camille and wondered if she'd go to her daddy after being traumatized by the doctor. I held her out to him, and thankfully she curled against his chest without any fuss. Savage reached down to take my hand and we walked down the sidewalk. Even though we'd gone shopping with Camille yesterday, today felt different. We felt like a real family. I didn't know if it was because my shock had worn off, or because Savage had finally made me his in truth. Possibly a bit of both.

We entered the diner and stepped to the side of the door while we waited to be seated. A few people eyed us with open curiosity, and two women across the room sneered at me. I hoped like hell Savage didn't notice. Something told me he wouldn't let anyone disrespect me.

A waitress came over with a smile on her face. "Sorry for the wait. You need a high chair for the cutie?"

"Yes, please," I said.

She grabbed two menus, a paper one with a scene to color, and a small pack of crayons, as well as three rolls of silverware. "Follow me."

She led us past the table with the ladies and stopped at a booth a few spots down. Savage slid into the booth with Camille and I took a seat across from them. The waitress placed everything on the table, then rushed off toward a back hall. She came back a moment later with a wooden high chair in her hands.

Savage transferred Camille to the seat and fastened her in while I got her menu and crayons ready for her. I had no idea if she'd actually use them, but it wouldn't hurt to try and get her interested in something.

"I'll take your drink order and return in a minute," the waitress said. "Oh, and my name's Molly."

"I'll have a sweet tea," I said, "and either milk or apple juice for our daughter."

"I'm afraid the juice is gone, but we do have milk." She smiled at Camille. "Such a little sweetheart."

"I'll have sweet tea like my wife," Savage said.

Wife? I stared at him a moment before turning

back to Camille. I didn't know why he'd called me that. We weren't married. I picked up a crayon and colored a small corner of her picture before handing another color to her. She reached out and took it, but didn't make a move to do anything else. I colored another small spot with her watching me intently. By the third small piece, she put the crayon against the paper and started to scribble.

"Savage, look," I said softly. "She's coloring."

He reached out and stroked her hair. Camille froze for a brief second before scribbling some more. It was the first time I'd seen her act like a regular kid, and I hoped it was a sign of more good things to come. Molly came back for our order and I scrambled to pick something off the list of Specials while Savage ordered for himself and got a grilled cheese for Camille.

Once she'd left again, I reached across the table to take Savage's hand. He linked our fingers together as we watched our daughter. She wore the blue crayon down to the paper, and I quickly handed her the green. I made sure she could reach the other colors and peeled a bit of paper off the blue one before setting it down.

One of the women who'd disliked me on sight stopped by the table on her way to the back hall. She huffed as she stared at the three of us before setting her gaze on Savage.

"You should be ashamed of yourself. Your wife is barely more than a child and you clearly got her pregnant when she was a teenager." The woman lifted her nose in the air, staring down at him. "You should be reported."

I felt my temper spark and my lips thinned. "Not that our lives are *any* of your business, but he saved me from being sold. So you can take your self-righteous attitude and shove it up your ass, you old bat! Learn to mind your own fucking business."

She gasped and clutched at her neck as she staggered back a step. "Why, I never!"

"Maybe that's the problem," I said. "You've never had someone tell you to shut the hell up. Savage didn't touch me until I'd turned eighteen. Camille is the daughter of my heart, but I'm the only mother she'll ever know. So thanks for bringing up something painful."

The woman stalked off and I heard a soft chuckle from Savage. I glared at him. The insufferable man winked at me.

Molly rushed over, wringing her hands. "I'm *so* sorry! I'd heard her whispering with her friend. It didn't occur to me she'd be so bold as to come over to your table."

Savage waved her off. "Not your job to control that woman's mouth or actions. There's plenty like her in the world. Besides, my wife put her in her place rather nicely."

Molly gave us a relieved smile. "Yes, she did. Do y'all need anything while you wait on your meal?"

"We're good," Savage said.

Molly ran off again, checking on her other tables. I noticed the woman who'd approached us sailed past without even glancing our way. Her friend's cheeks were flushed, and she wouldn't make eye contact with me. They were old enough to know better than to gossip about other people, much less say something so awful to Savage. I wanted to rip their hair out.

"I can't believe that woman," I muttered.

"We'll run into more like her," he said, squeezing my fingers. "You really think I saved you?"

"If you hadn't claimed me, I'm not sure where

I'd have ended up. My dad might have gotten me away from Ty. He might not have gotten there in time and I could be someone's sex slave right now. Or whatever the hell they wanted me for. So yeah, you saved me, whether you think so or not."

He smiled a little. "I think you're the one who saved me. I hadn't planned to settle down. Relationships don't go so well for me. When the Dixie Reapers needed someone to step in and claim you, I thought it might be my chance to have someone in my life."

I opened my mouth to ask what the hell he meant about his past relationships when Molly brought out food to the table. I unrolled my silverware and stabbed at my food like it had offended me. I waited until Molly walked off before making my first, and possibly only, demand of Savage.

"When we get home, we're talking about this. I think you owe me that much."

He nodded and looked like I'd just kicked his puppy, if he'd had one. I wondered what he'd been hiding from me. It made me realize I knew very little about his past. I'd gotten to know him a bit over the last year. It didn't hit me until just now that he'd never talked about his younger years. Had he been in love before? Had he been married at some point? I didn't like the way I felt, thinking of him in the arms of another woman. Sure, I'd known he'd been with club whores, but I didn't count them. I knew damn well none of the bikers respected them.

I ate a few bites before realizing Camille struggled with her sandwich. I broke it into small pieces and watched a moment to make sure she could chew and swallow without choking, then went back to attacking my food.

Something told me this day was only going to get worse.

* * *

Savage

It had been foolish to think I'd never have to talk to Mariah about Ellie. I'd wanted her to stay dead and buried, not have her ghost standing between us. I kept thinking back over my words at the diner and knew this was my own damn fault. I'd alluded to past relationships, and now Mariah was pissed. Not once in any of our conversations had I mentioned anyone special in my life. Now I'd waved the red flag in front of the proverbial bull, and Mariah looked ready to rip my balls off.

If I'd thought lunch had been tense, dinner had been worse. She'd softened a little when Doolittle brought the kittens over. Camille had loved them, just as we'd predicted. In fact, when she'd gone to bed twenty minutes ago, the kittens had curled up with her. We'd left her door open and put up the baby gate one of the Prospects had dropped off earlier. I'd already watched the kittens climb over it twice, so I knew they wouldn't be trapped without a litter box. But it would keep Camille from wandering.

I sat in my favorite chair with a beer while Mariah sat across from me on the couch. She'd put as much space between us as she could. How the hell did I even start this conversation? Ellie was the last thing I wanted to talk about. Now, or ever. She'd ripped me to shreds and made me question everything I'd thought I'd known about myself.

"How many relationships have you had?" she asked. "And the whores don't count."

I winced, thankful I at least didn't have to tell her

about how many of those women I'd been with. Since she'd grown up with the Dixie Reapers, she'd known what to expect. She wouldn't hold those women against me, as long as I didn't put my dick in any of them now. I had a feeling Mariah would gut me in my sleep if I cheated on her. Some clubs didn't believe in being faithful to their old ladies, but the Devil's Fury were different. All right. Maybe not too different since I knew at least a half dozen clubs or more just like ours. We didn't walk the straight and narrow, but there were some lines we didn't cross. Cheating on our women was one of them.

"One," I said.

"One?" Her brow furrowed. "But you said…"

"Right. Relationships plural, except I only ever had one girlfriend. The other women were all one-night stands or club whores. The only time I tried to give everything I had to a woman, she destroyed me."

Mariah shifted and seemed to relax a little. "Tell me about her. Please."

I sighed and took a swallow of my beer. "Her name was Ellie, and she was my high-school sweetheart. Or I'd thought she was."

It took an hour to pour out every detail of my time with Ellie, and how she'd killed herself as a way to escape being with me. Not only did the story make me look like a complete idiot, but the fact I'd never tried to claim another woman also made me look weak. As far as my brothers knew, I just hadn't found anyone worth keeping, until now.

Mariah stood and came closer, placing a knee on either side of my thighs and bracing her hands on my shoulders. When I looked into her eyes, I saw compassion and understanding. It gutted me. I'd thought Ellie had killed some part of me. With Mariah,

I knew if she walked away, nothing else would matter anymore. I'd just be going through the motions day-to-day, and I'd never be able to replace her. The way she'd stood by my side when I found out about Camille, the trusting way she'd given herself to me last night... There wasn't another woman like her in all the world, and she was mine.

"Ellie didn't deserve you," she said before kissing me. "I'm sorry she wasn't stronger. She should have told you how she felt, but I think there must have been something else going on. That was a flimsy excuse to end her life, Savage, and you damn well know it. She was hurting, probably felt isolated or like no one cared, and she decided to end it all. That's on her and not you. She clearly needed help and didn't want to ask for it or didn't know how. You can't punish yourself forever for someone else's actions."

"Her family hated me."

"They were wrong to place the blame on your shoulders, but they probably couldn't handle the idea their daughter had wanted to die. They couldn't face the knowledge they should have seen something was wrong with her, so they made you the scapegoat. Can you imagine if you woke one morning and found out Camille had ended her life? You'd lash out at other people, right?"

I cupped her cheek, the tension inside me loosening at her words. I hadn't ever considered it from her parents' point of view. They'd lost their child, and it had been too painful or traumatic, so they'd pointed their fingers at me. I hadn't made Ellie kill herself, even though she'd left a note claiming she'd seen no other way out of her relationship with me. I'd never forced her to be with me. Her death had hit me hard. Not only because I'd cared about her, but because I'd felt responsible.

"You're too good to me, Mariah. There are times you're so damn sweet and have an innocence in your eyes, and other times you act far wiser than anyone your age should be. I'm damn lucky to call you mine, and don't think I don't realize that."

"I wish you'd told me about Ellie before. You don't have to keep things like that from me, Savage. I accept you as you are. You know that, right?"

"Yeah, sweetheart. I know." I ran my fingers through her hair. "Guess I wasn't ready for you to see that part of me yet. It wasn't something I'm proud of."

She leaned in closer. "I won't say it again, so listen close. It. Wasn't. Your. Fault."

"You're amazing, you know that?" I tugged her closer and kissed her, taking my time. Mariah melted against me, her breasts flush with my chest. My cock went rock hard almost instantly, and I hoped like hell she wasn't sore from last night.

"Our daughter is asleep," she murmured against my lips. "And she can't escape her room."

"What exactly are you saying? I don't want any miscommunication between us. Especially if sex is involved."

She kissed my lips. My cheek. Then nipped my neck. "I'm saying you can take me right here and now. I don't always need a bed. Sometimes being spontaneous might be fun."

I gripped her hips tighter and shifted her until I knew my cock pressed against her pussy. "I will give you what you want anytime and anywhere."

A smile curled her lips. "Anywhere? Really? I somehow doubt that."

I paused. Her words making me wonder exactly where she'd want me to fuck her. I knew I was too damn possessive to let anyone watch, much less participate. Was that something she wanted? Taking the club whores in the middle of the clubhouse was one thing. Those women weren't mine. They scratched an itch and nothing more. But Mariah was my woman, and I damn sure didn't want anyone else seeing her naked.

"Someplace you had in mind?" I asked, needing to know.

She shook her head. "I'm not into exhibitionism, if that's what you were thinking. But you did say anywhere, and I seriously doubt you'd take me out in the open where anyone could walk by."

"No, I don't like the idea of other men seeing what's mine. The fact that cop had his hands on you is bad enough."

"Can we make a deal?" she asked.

"Depends. What is it?"

"You don't bring up my time with Ty, and I won't bring up Ellie or the club whores."

I winced. I hadn't realized I mentioned him that frequently. I fucking hated that he'd touched her first, even if I'd been the one to take her virginity. No doubt it made me a caveman, but the thought of him being with her, kissing her, putting his hands on her body, it made me want to rip him to shreds.

"I'm sorry, Mariah. It wasn't intentional."

She cupped my cheek. "I know."

"Guess I ruined the moment," I said, hugging her to me.

"I wouldn't say it's ruined, but yes, it did put a damper on things. You could change that, though."

I gripped her hair and tugged her head back. "How?"

"I like it when you get bossy and demanding."

She licked her lips. "When you told me what to do in the bedroom last night, it made me wet."

I tugged on her hair again. "What else did you like?"

"Being tied up. And what you're doing now."

"Yeah?" I pulled her hair a little harder. "I noticed you also liked having your nipples pinched. Does my girl like a little pain with her pleasure? Maybe a tiny bit?"

"Yes." She moaned, squeezing me with her thighs. "I liked all of it."

"Me pinning you down and making you take my cock?" I asked, then wanted to take the words back. I'd hurt her, even though I hadn't meant to. But she surprised me and nodded, her eyes getting darker with arousal. "That it, baby? You want me to bind your hands, pin you down, and do whatever I want to you? Make you suck my cock?"

"Yes," she said in a near whisper.

I brought her closer and made my voice deeper. "Put my cock in any hole I want? You going to lie there like a good girl and take it? Maybe even beg for more?"

"Oh, God." Her eyes closed and I felt her shudder. She ground against my cock, her hips jerking right before she cried out. *Holy shit*! Had she just come?

"Baby, baby, baby." I made a tsking sound. "That was extra naughty. Getting off without permission? Stand up and take off your clothes."

I released her and she scrambled off my lap, yanking at her clothing. It fell to the floor one piece at a time, then she stood in front of me, waiting for further instructions. I took in the soft curves of her body, her pert breasts, and her hard nipples. One of these days, I'd get someone to watch Camille, and I'd spend all day fucking my woman. I wanted to worship every inch of her.

I spread my thighs a little and patted one. "Over my lap, Mariah. I think you've earned a spanking."

It looked like her legs nearly buckled, but she hastened to obey. Her hands gripped the denim covering my leg and I smoothed my hand over her ass cheeks. I dipped my fingers between her thighs and felt how slick her pussy was already.

"I think coming without permission earns you five spankings. And, baby, I won't be going easy on you. I want to see this ass turn red. I'll be feeling the heat off your skin when I'm finished. Understand?"

"Yes, Gates."

At least she remembered to use my real name. I didn't mind her calling me by my road name, except when we were having sex. It was too personal for her to use anything but my given name during those times. She wasn't a club whore, or some faceless, nameless one-night stand I'd never remember. She was mine.

I brought my hand down on her ass with a loud *crack*. She yelped and jolted. I placed my forearm across her back to hold her still, spanking her again. Her skin had already turned a bright pink and was warming. I smacked her ass again, the next three strokes coming in rapid succession and each one harder than the last. She cried out and I knew she felt the burn, and a little pain. Nothing to cause lasting harm to her. Although it might be a bit tender for her to sit tomorrow. Especially if she earned any more spankings.

"Spread your legs, Mariah. Show me how wet you are." She obeyed quickly, and I rubbed my fingers along her slick folds. I stroked her clit once, softly, before backing off. She protested at the loss, and I brought my hand down on her ass again. "I decide when you can come, Mariah. Stand up."

She stood and I did as well. I pulled my belt free of the loops on my jeans, cracked the leather together once, then reached for her. I wrapped it around her wrists, securing her. Then I led her to the front entry. She'd probably never noticed the hook behind the door. I'd hung my cut there more than a few times.

Tonight, I used it to anchor her hands, looping the leather belt over the hook. It stretched her body, and I took a moment to admire the view. Pulling out my phone, I snapped a picture of her. No one would ever see it but me. Just knowing it was on my phone would tempt me every time I was away from her. And if I got sent on an overnight trip, or longer, I'd use it to jerk off.

I fisted her hair, pulling her head back. "Spread your legs."

She parted her thighs and went up on her tiptoes. I gripped her hip with one hand, holding on her hair still with my other. I rubbed against her ass and licked the length of her neck.

I let go of her hip long enough to unfasten my pants. I pushed them down far enough to free my cock, then lined up with her pussy and thrust hard and deep.

"Gates!" Her pussy clenched down hard and I felt the gush of her release.

"Did my baby need to be fucked?" I asked. "Because you came again without permission. How needy are you, Mariah?"

"So needy," she said, whining a little. "Please. Please fuck me."

"I'm not feeling very gentle. Can you handle me?"

She nodded and it was all I needed from her. I

pinned her body between mine and the wall and started driving into her. It was fast. Hard. Deep. And damn near savage, just like my fucking name. Less than a dozen strokes and I was coming inside her, filling her up with my cum, and still I fucked her. My cock didn't soften even a little.

I shifted my angle, hitting just the right spot, and she came again. I pulled another two orgasms from her before I found my second release. I didn't fill her with nearly as much cum the second time, but at least my dick didn't stay stiff. I withdrew from her body and watched as the thick white fluid slid down her thighs.

"Keep your legs open." I nipped her ear. "I'm going to take a picture of your pussy covered in my cum. It's a fucking beautiful sight."

I held my phone at the right angle to get the best picture and snapped two before putting the device back in my pocket. I unhooked Mariah's hands and released her from the leather belt. Her knees buckled and I quickly lifted her into my arms. Thankfully my pants remained far enough up I could carry her to our room. I just hoped like fuck Camille wasn't awake and watching as we went past, since her mom was definitely naked.

I nudged the bedroom door mostly shut with my foot before placing Mariah on the bed. It didn't take but a minute for me to strip out of my clothes, then I crawled in next to her. She started to get up and I put a hand on her belly, holding her down.

"Gates, I need to clean up."

I arched an eyebrow at her. "No, you don't. You're going to lie here with my cum smeared across your pussy lips and on your thighs. And when I get my second wind, I'm going to flip you over and fuck you again. Or maybe I'll have you ride me so I can watch you."

She sighed and snuggled closer. "Fine. If more orgasms are coming my way, then I'll stay messy. But if my thighs get glued together because you wouldn't let me clean up, I'm not going to be happy with you."

I kissed her and held her close. Even though I knew I couldn't keep her up all night, not when we had Camille to worry about, there was no way in hell I'd sleep without having her at least once more. The woman was like a drug, and I couldn't get enough of her.

Chapter Nine

Mariah

I watched Camille as she plucked flowers, otherwise known as weeds called oxalis, to make a bouquet. Every time I moved, I wanted to cry. It had been three weeks since Savage took my virginity, and he'd fucked me every night since them, usually more than once. My pussy hurt and so did my ass, since he kept spanking me. As soon as Camille took a nap, I needed to soak in a hot bath, and I needed to learn how to say no to Savage.

I couldn't complain, in all honesty. I loved everything we did in the bedroom -- or the living room, kitchen, bathroom... no room had been off limits except Camille's and the hallway. At least I no longer worried there might be another woman. He spent far more time at home now. If the President hadn't called Church, he'd likely be out here with us. He enjoyed watching Camille explore as much as I did.

She'd healed a bit since being here. I could hug her, or bathe her, without seeing her flinch or scream in fear. She even let Savage change her clothes or help her in the bath. Strangers still presented a problem, but I hoped with time, she'd get over her fears and learn to trust again. As far as I knew, no one had any information on what happened to Camille. If Savage had learned anything, he hadn't shared it with me.

Camille toddled over and handed me the flowers she'd picked. I smiled and kissed her cheek in thanks. She grinned at me and went to find more. The sound of a motorcycle drew my attention, but it wasn't Savage. I saw Van pull up and park on the street. He walked over, keeping an eye on Camille to make sure she didn't freak, then sat on the step next to me.

"Should I be concerned?" I asked. "You're here, sitting close to me, and aren't scanning the area to make sure Savage isn't about to rip you apart."

"He asked me to come."

Now he had my attention. I turned partially to face him. "What the hell does that mean?"

"The case against Officer Clarke was thrown out this morning. He's in the wind. The hackers are searching the local cameras to locate him. Far as we know, he can't find you. Anything more than that, you'll have to ask Savage. I've already said more than I probably should have, but Savage agreed I could tell you the basics. He wanted to make sure you didn't run off."

I motioned to the empty driveway. "With what transportation? Someone took the club truck this morning and he hasn't bought me anything yet."

"He's worried about you, Mariah. He went from only having the club, to having a woman and kid." He glanced at Camille. "You should ask him what he's heard about her situation. I didn't get to listen to everything, but I overheard a bit. I'm surprised she's doing as well as she is."

I took a breath, trying to steady myself. I wanted to scream. To rage at the world for allowing men like Ty to exist, much less monsters who preyed on children. Those sick fucks needed to be six feet under, and I hoped like hell Savage found whoever had hurt our daughter and made them suffer.

"Am I on lockdown?" I asked. "Should I take Camille back inside?"

"I think we're far enough from the fence line you should be okay. I won't promise no one will slip inside. Every time the club thinks they've ensured no one can breach the compound, some asshole comes along and proves them wrong."

"But everyone knows to watch for Ty?" I asked. "They've seen his picture and won't let him through the gates, right? Not even if he shows up with a badge and demands entry?"

"We know what the fucker looks like. He's not getting past any of us." He smiled as Camille toppled over trying to reach another flower. "She's cute. Savage mentioned she's deaf. Has anyone tried to talk to her with sign language?"

I blinked in surprise. "Um, no. I don't know it and I'm not sure about Savage."

"Mind if I try?" he asked.

"You know sign language?"

He nodded. "My mom was deaf. She wasn't born that way. Got into a bad accident as a kid and lost her hearing."

"Be my guest. If she knows sign language, I'll need you to teach me. Or least get me going and I'll look for another way to learn."

He stood and approached Camille, hunkering down a few feet from her. I knew the moment she realized he'd walked up to her. She froze, staring at the ground. Van waved his hand in her line of sight, and she jerked her head up. He gave her a charming smile and started signing something.

Camille plopped onto her butt and started crying. I started to rise and run to her, but I noticed her little hands were moving. Her movements weren't as smooth as Van's had been, but it was clear she was communicating with him.

Van inched closer and held out his hands. Camille crawled over and let him hug her. My heart ached. All this time she knew how to talk to us. We'd let her down. It had never occurred to me she might have a different way of communicating. Did that mean I was already failing at being her mom?

I walked over and sank to my knees next to them. "What did she say?"

"She was overwhelmed, I think. I'm not sure where she learned it. Did her aunt use sign language at all while she was here dropping off Camille?"

"No, but it wouldn't surprise me if she'd have kept that hidden. If she thought Savage would deny an imperfect child, she'd have omitted the part about Camille not being able to hear. I only discovered it by looking through the file she'd left."

"Let's get her inside. We can sit with her while I teach you a few things. I think she needs to see you're trying to speak with her. If she's watching you, she'll see your lips move and as she gets older, she'll possibly learn to read lips. My mom could as long as someone didn't talk too fast."

Camille let him carry her into the house, and I made sure to lock the door behind me. Knowing Ty was out there somewhere made a chill skate down my spine. Would he blame me for being locked up? Clearly it hadn't done any good since they'd set him free. He wouldn't be able to lure in any new girls, not as long as he lived in the same town. Everyone would be watching him now, especially the Chief of Police.

I hated not feeling completely safe in my own home.

I sank to the floor in Camille's room while she played with some blocks. Van sat across from me. As he spoke, he used his hands to sign everything. He went slow so I could pick up on at least a few things. I saw the way Camille's eyes lit up when she realized what I was doing. I'd have to tell Savage we had a way to communicate with our daughter, but it would require both of us to learn another language.

It would take time to learn enough to talk to Camille as easily as I would if I could use my words. I didn't know if her hearing loss was permanent, but if someone had taken the time to teach a toddler how to use sign language, I had to wonder if the doctor had already determined she'd never hear. I hadn't seen that part in the notes. Of course, the file hadn't had nearly as much information as I'd have liked. Clearly Bethany had given us the bare minimum when she'd dropped off Camille.

A fist pounded on the front door and I jolted. Van placed a hand on my knee.

"Stay here. I'll see who it is," he said.

The sound must have startled the kittens. They both ran into Camille's room and straight to her. It looked like my new daughter had two pets. The furry terrors tolerated me and knew I fed them, but otherwise they preferred her company. I considered the fact animals seemed to be so in tune with their surroundings as well as the emotions of those around them. Maybe they knew she needed them more than I did.

I heard the heavy tread of two sets of feet and a moment later both Van and Savage stepped into view. I stood and rushed over to them, throwing my arms around Savage. He held me close and brushed a kiss to the top of my head.

"It was smart to lock the door," he said. "I grabbed my bike key this morning and didn't think to take the set with the house key on it."

"Van told me Ty is out of jail."

"Yeah. I'll tell you what I can. Badger would like to keep you in the dark about a few things, but I think you can handle it. You're a Reaper's daughter, after all."

I nodded.

"Want me to take Camille over to Farrah's house? I'll stay with her, but she might like to play with Rebel," Van said.

I felt the hesitation in Savage, but he hadn't learned the latest about his daughter. I smiled at Van and told him to go ahead. "I think Savage and I need a little quiet time to discuss a few things, including Camille."

Van scooped her up and left the house. I took Savage's hand and led him to the kitchen, where I brewed a pot of coffee. I didn't drink it often. Today called for something stronger than sweet tea. Hell, he might want to add a bit of rum to the cup. I couldn't remember seeing him look so haggard. It made me wonder exactly what had been said during Church.

"First, you should know Camille can have a conversation with someone, just not with words," I said.

"Explain."

"She knows sign language. Van apparently learned it from his mom and decided to see if Camille would recognize any words he signed to her. She seems to know quite a bit, and he started teaching me a few things. We'll both need to learn. I have a feeling this means her hearing loss is permanent."

Savage ran a hand through his hair. "Christ. I'd hoped she could hear eventually. The world is dangerous enough already without her not having all her senses. We'll both learn it together. I want to be able to talk to my daughter."

The coffeemaker chirped and I poured us each a cup, then took the seat next to him. I waited until he'd had a few swallows before I decided to ask about Ty.

The more I knew, the better prepared I could be. Each of us had taken lessons with Tank on how to defend ourselves. I just hadn't realized I needed to fight off Ty. He'd been so smooth, luring me in with sweet words and kisses. I'd completely missed the signs.

"So, Ty is free. What does that mean for me?" I asked.

"Right now, nothing. Far as we can tell, he has no clue where you are, and I'd like to keep it that way. Which means your dad will be keeping his distance for the moment. Although, I did ask about your sister. If Ty knew Farrah lived here, he might assume you came to stay with her."

Shit. I couldn't remember what I'd told him about Farrah. "He knows she moved to another state, but I'm not sure if I ever told him exactly where she lived."

"Wire and Lavender are already monitoring his calls, texts, and emails. Your dad's club also has eyes on him. Not any of their own, but apparently Casper VanHorne suggested a few discreet people. They blend well and shouldn't be detected."

"Well, if those two and Casper are working together, then I don't think he'll be much of an issue. Do we know for sure yet if he's been working alone?" I asked.

"He has a partner in town. Not at the police department. It's a guy in the mayor's office. Looks like your dad's club spent all that time cleaning house only for corruption to seep back in. From what Wire said, they're gathering as much info as they can on all the players, or the ones they can find. After that, either Chief Daniels will handle it, or since that didn't go very well before, he may decide to go visit his daughter and turn a blind eye for a few days while the Dixie Reapers handle business."

I chewed on my bottom lip. I loved my dad, and Torch, but both were getting up there. A lot of the patched members and officers were. Even Wire was in his forties now, which made him close to Savage in age. If I didn't balk at my man going after the bad guys, it made me a bit hypocritical to say my dad's club shouldn't. But still... If they were going after human traffickers, which I knew they'd done years if not decades ago, I hoped they let the younger guys take this one. I didn't want my dad, Torch, Bull, or anyone else their ages going after these guys. Not that I'd ever tell them. It would hurt their pride.

"You're worried," Savage said.

"My dad isn't exactly as young as he was when he saved my mom. Same for my grandfather. And Torch..." I sighed. "I don't want to dent their egos, but I wish they'd let the younger guys take this one."

Savage leaned back in his seat, sprawling a little. The way he eyed me didn't bode well. I could see the tic in his jaw, telling me I'd pissed him off.

"You realize your dad isn't exactly some paper pusher working an eight-to-five job in a cushy office building, right? He might be getting closer to sixty, but the man can still hold his own. Torch is only a handful of years older than him. Trust them to get the job done, baby. And don't ever let them know you doubted they were capable of handling business."

I sighed and twisted the coffee cup in my hands. "I'm allowed to worry. If you went after these men, I'd worry about you too. It's not that I don't think any of you can't protect yourselves, or me, I just wish you didn't have to. There are guys closer to my age eager to jump into the fray, and Prospects just waiting to prove themselves. Why can't they handle it?"

He reached over and gripped my chin, lifting my face until I held his gaze. "Your dad will do his damnedest to return home every time he leaves the house, because he has your mom, your brother, your sister, you, and his granddaughters, even if he hasn't had a chance to meet our daughter yet. Just like I'll fight like hell to return home no matter what situation I'm in, because I want to be here with you and Camille. Understand?"

"I know." I reached up and wrapped my fingers around his wrist. "I care about you. All of you. The thought of any of you not making it back absolutely guts me."

He pulled me into his lap and kissed me softly. "Badger is going to send two men to help your dad's club. Since you're mine, and Farrah belongs to Demon, that makes the Reapers our family in a sense. Which is why Beast is sending someone as well, since Lyssa belongs to him and Danica is Ranger's. Not to mention Chief Daniel's daughter is the old lady to the Reckless Kings VP. They aren't going after these men alone, all right?"

"But you're staying here?" I asked.

"For now. Once the issue with Ty is handled, I'll go after the people who hurt Camille."

I leaned into him. "Can you tell me anything? I can't help her if I don't know exactly what I'm fighting against."

"It's not pretty. You sure you can stomach it? I caught you bawling your eyes out before we had any idea what she'd been through with any certainty."

"Tell me. She's my daughter too, Savage. I'll be strong -- for her."

He nodded and tightened his hold on me. "All right. You know her mom was a club whore. Outlaw and Surge worked together to check into Destiny and her cousin Bethany, as well as look for anything on Camille. Destiny must have known she was pregnant when she left here. She didn't take off because she was scared. At least, that's what we're assuming. I think she knew we'd keep Camille, then she wouldn't be able to use her as currency.

"Camille was only a year old the first time Destiny sold her for an hour to a man, in exchange for drugs. It was something common the man did, and he left a paper trail. It wasn't easy to find, but Surge managed to uncover it. He kept a detailed record, as well as videos and pictures, of his time with the kids he abused."

I put my hand over my mouth in horror. "Oh, God. Savage, was Camille... did he have... I..."

"Yeah, baby. He had some pictures of Camille and videoed his first time with her. I'm not going to tell you the details. I wish like fuck I didn't know them. There's a reason she freaked over having her mouth touched by the doctor, and why she doesn't like people to touch her when she isn't dressed, especially men. But Destiny was a sick fucking bitch and didn't care if she sold my daughter to men or women."

"I think I'm going to be sick." I struggled to get off his lap and rushed for the trash can, throwing up everything in my stomach.

After I finished, I rinsed my mouth and closed my eyes, trying to blot out the images dancing through my mind of what our sweet baby girl had suffered. "You have all their names?"

"Yeah, I do."

"And Bethany?" I asked.

"She didn't sell her, but there's a reason she brought Camille here, and it didn't have anything to do with her mental health. To be fair, she really has been institutionalized three times for depression and once for attempted suicide. But she hightailed it straight to our gates within hours of receiving a call from one of Camille's main abusers. It seems Destiny gave up her daughter's location before she died."

"Wait. I'm confused."

"I told you Destiny was dead. She'd been tortured and dumped on the side of the road. At first, I'd wondered if it could be somehow tied into the human trafficking ring Officer Clarke was part of, even if it did seem farfetched. One of the men who paid for Camille at least once a week tortured Destiny, on video, to get the location of my daughter. Then he handed her off to men who prefer hurting women. She didn't go easy."

I shivered and went back to Savage, crawling into his lap. If there was ever a time I needed to be held, it was now. He wrapped his arms around me, and I snuggled in.

There were times I hated our world. It was so dark and ugly, and yet it had beauty too. People would look at Savage or my dad and see a bad person, but they fought for those who couldn't stand up for themselves.

"So we just sit and wait?" I asked.

"For the moment. Wire said he and Lavender would have everything turned over to Torch by morning. They'll most likely go after the men in the next few days. I'd prefer you not go anywhere near the fence line or the gates. If they can't see you, they won't know for certain if you're here."

"I understand. Not my first rodeo."

He chuckled. "No, I guess it's not. And clearly you used to hang out with Danica. Rodeo? Really?"

I shrugged. "Fine. Not my first... Hell, I don't even know what else to say. Gunfight? War?"

"When I know you're safe, I'm going to focus on the people who hurt Camille. The man who abused her the worst is mine. That fucker is going to suffer, and I won't let him die easy. The others I'll let the hackers destroy. They're already prepping a file to send to the FBI. Those men and women will be rotting in federal prison, and once word gets out they're child molesters and rapists, they'll get a taste of their own medicine."

"And I'm guessing someone will make sure the other prisoners find out why they're in there."

"Yep. I've been guaranteed it will happen." He hugged me tight. "Camille wasn't raped. In case you wondered. I'm not sure she'd have survived it if she had been. Doesn't lessen the trauma she suffered, but at least she was spared that much."

"Why is evil allowed to exist? They're like a freakin' hydra. You cut off the head of one and three more grow back. For every monster your club, my dad's, or the others have taken down, more pop up. It's never-ending and feels like it's getting worse instead of better."

He ran his hand up and down my thigh. "The world has always had men like the ones who wanted to sell you, and the people who hurt Camille. The difference is technology makes it easier to spread the word about them. Not to mention, as the population grows, the odds increase that evil will spread. Some people are just born bad, baby. Nothing we can do about it."

"I know. It just sucks."

I refused to live every second of my life looking over my shoulder, but I'd definitely pay more attention to the people getting close to me. And heaven help anyone who came after Camille now that she was mine.

Savage wouldn't get a chance to take them down because I'd tear them apart for daring to touch her.

Chapter Ten

Savage

I couldn't place what had woken me at first, until the sounds of retching reached my ears. I bolted from the bed and went into the bathroom. Mariah hugged the toilet, emptying the contents of her stomach. I tried to think if anyone had been sick lately. She hadn't left the compound, so if she'd caught a bug, one of us had to have given it to her. I hunkered down beside her and rubbed her back.

"You need some water, baby?" I asked.

She whimpered so I took that as a no. I kept using firm, long strokes up and down her back. She finally seemed to have purged everything and sat back. I wet a cloth and wiped her face, then helped her stand. She brushed her teeth, leaning heavily against me.

"What's wrong, Mariah? Just upset stomach?"

"Think so," she murmured. "I was dead asleep and suddenly woke feeling like I would puke up my guts. Think I did that and then some."

"Want me to see if the doctor would be willing to come here?" I asked. "Your dad and the others were closing in on the human trafficking ring, but they didn't have everyone as of last night. I don't want to risk you leaving the compound just yet."

"It's probably just a bug. I don't want Camille to catch it, or you. Better keep your distance."

I hugged her, and something on the counter caught my attention. "When's the last time you needed the tampons?"

She tensed and looked over her shoulder at the box before meeting my gaze. "Um. Not since before Camille came to live with us. Like maybe three or four weeks before."

My eyebrows rose as I did the math. She hadn't had her period in at least a month and a half. "Think you could be pregnant?"

She pressed a hand to her belly and seemed to consider it. After a moment, she nodded. "Yeah. It's possible. I've always been pretty regular with my cycle. Stress can delay it or even make me skip, but considering my morning trip to the bathroom the last two mornings..."

"What?" I took a step back. "Two mornings? And you didn't say anything?"

"I didn't think much of it yesterday. We've all been under so much pressure between Ty and his cohorts and the people who hurt Camille, plus whatever else has everyone around here so busy, I thought it was a one-off thing. Until this morning. I was thinking it was a stomach virus until you mentioned my period."

"Want to take a test and find out?" I asked.

"You're going to ask a Prospect, aren't you?"

I grinned. "Yep. I'll have him get three different kinds. Go lie down and rest until he drops them off."

I kissed her forehead and helped her into bed. After a quick text to Van, I went to check on Camille, double-checked the rest of the house and the kittens, before kicking back in my favorite chair while I waited. A soft knock at the door sounded about twenty minutes later and I let Van in. He handed the sack to me and nearly ran from the house.

"Chickenshit," I called out after him before shutting the door and locking it. One day he'd knock up some girl, and then he'd be the one asking for pregnancy tests.

I carried the sack to the bathroom and set each

box out. I read the instructions before waking Mariah. She murmured sleepily but let me lead her into the bathroom. The fact she hadn't fully woken worked in my favor. I had a feeling she'd have pitched a fit about me standing here while she peed if she'd been more alert.

I had her take all three tests and set a timer. She didn't even stick around to wait for the results, which told me she'd been sleeping harder than I'd thought. It concerned me she'd been able to fall back to sleep so hard in such a short time. I'd have to make sure she got plenty of rest in the upcoming weeks. Even longer if she was pregnant like I thought.

The minutes dragged by and the timer finally went off. Every last one had a positive result. I grinned so big my cheeks hurt as I hurried back into the bedroom. I slid into bed and gathered her in my arms, kissing her awake.

"Tired," she mumbled.

"Don't you want to know what the tests said?"

She blinked like a sleepy owl. "Tests?"

"Yep. You just peed on three sticks. All of them came back positive."

She bolted upright and looked toward the bathroom, then back at me. "How... What... Savage! I was asleep!"

"You woke up enough to pee, then went back to bed. I'm not going to feel bad about it. You ready to expand our family?"

"We just found out we have a daughter and we're already adding another baby." She pushed her hair out of her face. "Can we handle two kids?"

"Little late now, Mariah. It's not like we can return either of them. They're ours and you know you'll love both of them. I've seen how you dote on

Camille. You think this one will be any different? You just have to go through the pain of giving birth this time."

She punched me in the arm, then shook her hand. "Why are you so hard? It's like hitting a damn rock!"

I smiled and tugged her back into my arms, kissing her. "Last I checked, you like it when I'm hard."

I rubbed my cock against her. If she hadn't been throwing up this morning, I'd take advantage of Camille being asleep. Finding out we were going to have a baby was cause for celebration. Couldn't think of a better way than making her scream in pleasure.

"Will you hate me if I say not right now?" she asked.

"No, baby. I wouldn't hate you. If you want to sleep some more, I'll just lie here and hold you." I pressed a kiss to her forehead. "You've made me so fucking happy, Mariah. Having Camille is amazing, but this time I get to be there from the very beginning. I'll go to every appointment with you and hold your hand when it's time to bring our baby into the world."

I felt her lips curl into a smile where she'd pushed her face against me. "You're awfully sappy for a big, tough biker. Good thing I grew up around a bunch of them and already knew you're all a bunch of marshmallows."

"Only with my girls."

I couldn't wait to share the news. As much as I wanted to grab my phone and send out a mass text to the club, I didn't dare. Not until Mariah had a chance to tell her sister and her parents. I wished I had family to call. My parents would have been shitty grandparents. It was probably a good thing they weren't around anymore.

Mariah slept as the sun started to filter through the windows. I heard Camille making noise in her room, and the kittens started meowing. I'd have loved to lie in bed with her all day, but the rest of the family needed my attention. I pulled the covers over her before slipping on a pair of sweatpants.

Camille stood at the gate across her door, waiting patiently. I lifted her into my arms and carried her to the bathroom. I checked her pull-up and noticed it had remained dry overnight.

"Such a good girl," I murmured, wishing she could hear me. I'd picked up a little sign language, but not enough to have a conversation with her. My sweet girl didn't get upset with me. We managed to communicate without words of any sort. Didn't mean I'd stop trying to learn. I hadn't had as much time to dedicate to picking up a new language with everything else going on. It was my first priority once all this was behind us.

I carried her to the kitchen and put her in the high chair. After I poured some food into the kittens' bowls and checked their water, I made some oatmeal for Camille. Coffee was a must so it was next on my list, then I sat and enjoyed some time with my little girl. She cleaned her bowl and I wiped off her face and hands. I took her to the bathroom again before letting her play in her bedroom.

Mariah kept her around while she cooked, and maybe one day I'd be confident enough to do that too, but for now I worried she'd get burned or wander off and get hurt while I wasn't paying attention. I didn't know how long Mariah would sleep. My stomach growled as I beat some eggs with a bit of milk. I added some diced peppers, tomatoes, and sliced up some leftover grilled chicken. Omelets were the one thing I could make without worrying about any mishaps -- like burning it.

I plated two of them and put both into the oven. It didn't seem right to eat without Mariah. No matter how tired she was, I didn't think she needed to sleep all day. I peeked into Camille's room and saw her playing with the kittens. When I got to the bedroom, Mariah wasn't in bed. I found her standing at the bathroom counter staring at the three test sticks.

"I didn't dream it?" she asked. "I'm really pregnant?"

"According to those, yes. I doubt three different types of tests would be wrong. We can schedule an appointment with the doctor next week."

She placed both hands over her flat stomach. "I can't believe there's a tiny human in here. We created a baby, Gates. It's going to be part you and part me. How amazing is that?"

I placed my hands on either side of the counter, pressing my chest to her back. "Pretty spectacular. You're already a wonderful mother. You've been so great with Camille. I haven't told anyone yet. I thought you'd want to share the news with your parents and sister first."

"I don't want to distract anyone right now." She leaned into me. "If my dad hears I'm pregnant, he could lose his focus. We can wait a little bit. But we could tell Camille she's going to be a big sister."

"How?" I asked.

"Get your phone. We'll look it up. Surely there's a YouTube or something on how to sign that."

I kissed her temple, then went to get my phone. It took a few minutes for us to master the hand motions, but once we'd figured it out, we went to tell

Camille. She stared at us at first, no emotion showing at all. I'd worried we'd done it wrong and double-checked the video. Then my little girl started to cry and it broke my fucking heart.

I hugged her to me, not knowing how to fix it.

"Call Van. I think we need help," I said.

While Mariah asked Van to come over, I rocked my daughter. Had it been a mistake to tell Camille about the baby? I wished I knew why she'd started crying. Did she think we were replacing her? Was she worried she wouldn't have a place here anymore? I hated not being able to talk to her.

"He said he's going to use FaceTime." Mariah turned so we could all see her screen. She accepted the call when it came through and Van waved. "Van, we told Camille that she's going to be a big sister, but I think the video we looked up must have been wrong. She started crying."

"First off, congrats! I know you must be excited. Now for Miss Camille." He signed something to Camille and her tears slowed. She paid attention to Van, who started to talk while he signed. "I hear you're going to be a big sister! Do you understand what that means?"

Camille signed something back to him and Van's face went tight before flushing with anger. He stopped signing. "She said her big sister let people hurt her. Guys, I don't think she knew Destiny was her mom."

Bethany had mentioned something about Camille not remembering Destiny. It had been a lie. She'd remembered that bitch, she just hadn't realized the woman was her mother. Thank God for small favors.

Van started talking to Camille again, signing as he spoke so we could understand too. "Big sisters are supposed to protect their little sisters and brothers. You'll get to teach them things, like how to sign, how to kick a ball, and other fun things. You'll be a good big sister. I can tell because you're so good with the kittens. They're like babies except with fur."

Camille signed something back and Van smiled at her. "That's right. You have your mom and dad to help you."

Her face scrunched up as she signed some more and Van held up a finger for us to wait while he disappeared. I heard him cussing and what sounded like his fist going through a wall before he came back.

"What the fuck?" I asked.

"She wanted to know why you hadn't wanted her before now. She thinks you left her with Destiny." Van shook his head before he started talking to Camille again. "Destiny hid you from your mom and dad. They didn't know where you were until your Aunt Bethany brought you here. They both love you so much, Camille. They were excited to tell you about the baby."

Camille snuggled into me and sighed. It seemed Van had eased her fears for the moment. If Destiny weren't dead, I'd kill the bitch myself. I knew it made me an asshole, but I was glad she'd suffered. Knowing what she'd done to Camille enraged me unlike anything I'd felt before. How could she have sold her own kid?

"I don't care if she gets mad at us later, no one better tell her I'm not her birth mother," Mariah said. "I'd rather she be upset when she's older than go through life thinking that piece of shit gave birth to her and could still hurt her that way. It's unforgiveable."

"Agreed," Van said. "She won't hear it from me."

"You were her mom the moment I claimed her as my daughter," I said. "Even she agreed. She called you momma from the very first. Doesn't matter if you carried her for nine months or not. You're her mom in every way that counts. Anyone says different, I'll knock their teeth down their throats."

Mariah put her head on my arm and reached up to run her fingers through Camille's hair. "Van, can you please tell her that I love her very much? I need her to know that she's wanted. Me having a baby doesn't change anything. She'll always be my little girl."

Van cleared his throat and quickly signed to Camille.

She pulled back from me and held her arms out to Mariah. "Ma-ma!"

Seeing the two of them, no one would ever question she and Mariah belonged together. It was clear they loved one another.

"Since you're the only one who can communicate with Camille, if I have to leave the house, I'd appreciate you staying with them. I'll let the club know I've asked you to be here in my absence. If something happens and Camille gets scared, I need you to calm her down. Mariah and I will keep teaching ourselves sign language, but we aren't proficient enough yet."

Van smiled. "Just stay off YouTube unless it's an academy or school for the deaf posting the videos. Otherwise, you may learn incorrectly and confuse Camille. I'm happy to help when I can. She's a little angel and spending time with her isn't a hardship."

"Thanks, Van. I'll remember this when it's time to vote you into the club."

He gave a nod. "I appreciate it, Savage. Just call if you need anything."

I ended the call and handed the phone back to Mariah. "Come on. I made you breakfast. Although, the omelets are probably cold by now."

"The microwave will warm them just fine," she said. "What about Camille?"

"She already had her oatmeal. Unless the club calls me away, I'm staying with the two of you until I know you're safe. Especially now."

She went up on tiptoe to kiss my cheek. "You're good to us, Savage. Just know I see you and everything you do not only for our club, but for our family too. I know the sacrifices you make."

"You and Camille are everything to me. I'd lay down my life for the both of you. Whatever it takes to keep you both safe."

I wrapped my arm around her and took comfort in having my two girls with me. Possibly three, if the little one we just found out about was a girl too. As much as I'd enjoy teaching a son how to ride a motorcycle, work on cars, and maybe one day see him patch into the club, having another girl would be just as amazing.

Maybe my daughters would like to learn those things too, even if they couldn't patch into the Devil's Fury. The club might have advanced a lot over the last several decades, but I didn't think it would ever reach the point of accepting women in the club as anything other than old ladies, daughters, or club whores. And my daughters sure the fuck wouldn't become that last one. Not as long as there was breath in my lungs.

Chapter Eleven
Mariah

"Mom, slow down! I can only understand every fifth word. What's going on?"

I checked on Camille again, making sure she hadn't gotten out of bed. Savage had been called away and Van lounged on the couch, flipping through the TV channels. Camille had been so excited about Van being in the house, I'd found her at the gate twice already, wanting to talk to Van one more time.

"I said Tyson Clarke got past the club. No one knows where he is, Mariah."

I paused. "All right. But he doesn't have any idea where *I* am. I don't think I ever told him where Farrah lived, so there's nothing linking me to the Devil's Fury."

"You don't understand. Wire and Lavender can't find him, Mariah. He's not showing on any cameras around town. He was there one second and gone the next. They think he found someone to hack into the systems, in which case Wire will eventually find them, but... it also means that person could have found a paper trail leading to you. Calls between us. Text messages."

I blew out a breath and went back to the living room. "Mom, I'm putting you on speaker. One of the Prospects is here with me. His name is Van. I need you to tell him everything you know."

Van stood, immediately on alert. I turned on the speaker and listened as Mom went through everything again. She answered Van's questions, but the longer she talked, the more uneasy I became. It seemed he'd not just disappeared in the last hour. He'd been missing long enough to make the drive from Alabama to Blackwood Falls, Georgia. If it was possible that Ty really did know where to find me, he wouldn't back down. There wasn't a single reason for him to come for me except either revenge, or his buyer still wanted me. Once he found out I wasn't a virgin anymore, I'd be useless to him. Unless he already knew. Mom thought he'd been reading our messages. All of them? Or just certain ones? Had I said anything to her about Savage finally claiming me completely? Phone conversations and text blurred together in my mind.

Pressing a hand to my belly, I silently prayed my baby wouldn't be harmed if anything happened. I didn't think I could handle that sort of loss, and I wasn't sure how Savage would react. I'd seen how excited he was about the baby, how happy. He'd already talked about setting up another room so Camille wouldn't have to share her space.

Van reached over to disconnect the call and I realized I'd zoned out. I should have known something would happen. My dad's club had been after Ty for nearly a week now. At first, they hadn't been able to find him at all. Then he'd popped up on camera around town. He'd eluded them every time. A vanishing act shouldn't have surprised me. He'd often gloated about how much smarter he was than everyone else in town, including his fellow officers. Of course, now it had a new context. I'd thought he'd just been showing off for me. Little had I realized he'd meant he was smarter than me too, because the asshole had tricked me.

"What now?" I asked.

"I'm going to make sure all the doors and windows are locked. I'll also text Savage and make sure he's aware Ty may be on his way here."

"You mean if he isn't here already? I think he

planned all this. He had to know he was being watched. This is his way of showing how stupid everyone is. He wanted us to know he has the upper hand."

Van reached out and squeezed my shoulder. "I'll keep you safe, Mariah. All three of you. I know I'm just a Prospect, but I've come to care about you and Camille. I'd even go so far as to call you a friend, if that's not too presumptuous."

I smiled. "I can always use friends, Van."

"He probably doesn't know about Camille. I wish I had a way to hide her. If Ty comes looking for you, he's not going to know the layout of the compound. Not even the locals are allowed to wander around in here. He'd need a brother or a Prospect to lead the way, and none of us would ever do that. We'd die before we let him have you."

"Right." I blew out a breath. "So, I'm safe. Mostly. Unless he decides to just kill anyone who gets in his way."

"Let's hope it doesn't come to that. I need you to pick a spot and stay there while I check the house. Where will you be?" he asked.

"I'll just sit here." I waved a hand at the couch. "Not sure my legs will keep holding me up for much longer. Please check on Camille again? She was sleeping a moment ago."

"I will."

He went to the window and checked it before moving to the front entry and doing the same with the door. I heard him move room to room, ensuring no one could get into the house unless they had a key. As far as I knew, there were only three keys. Mine, Savage's, and the one Demon had. He'd have to break down the door, or break a window, to get in because I damn sure wasn't going to invite him inside.

Now would have been an excellent time to have that massive underground safe house Tank had built for the Dixie Reapers. A knock sounded at the door. I tensed, fighting the instant response to get up and answer it. When no one called out a greeting, my stomach knotted. I glanced at the hallway, wondering why Van hadn't come to check it out.

The knock came again. Louder.

"Where are you, Van?" I whispered to myself. I didn't hear a single sound from the back of the house.

The door rattled on its hinges as someone pounded on it. I wasn't about to ask who was there and give away not only my location, but verify I was in the house. For all I knew, if it was Ty out there, he was only guessing I was here. Like Van said, there was no way he could know which house belonged to Savage. For that matter, he couldn't know where to find Farrah either.

"Come out, come out, wherever you are," a deep voice said from the front porch. "Or let me in."

I didn't recognize his voice. It wasn't Ty, so if he'd found me, he'd brought company. And seriously? Come out or let me in? Did he think I was born yesterday? No one could be that stupid, right? Nope. I would sit here and wait for Van.

"This is where you tell him not by the hair of your chinny chin chin." Ty smirked as he came into view. "Surprised to see me?"

I steeled my spine, refusing to flinch away from him. I wouldn't give him the satisfaction. He'd come from the back of the house. Where Van had gone. I hoped the Prospect was all right, and that Ty hadn't noticed Camille. If he'd seen her, I hoped he didn't decide to use her as leverage.

"How did you get in?"

He pulled out a knife and flicked open the blade, waving it in the air. "One of your bedroom windows doesn't latch tightly. It was easy enough to use this to wiggle the locking mechanism until I could come in."

"What do you want, Ty?"

"Want?" His gaze skimmed over me, lingering on my breasts. "A man can't come get his fiancée? We had plans, Mariah. You missed our wedding."

So we were playing *that* game. Surely by now he knew I was on to him? He didn't really think I'd just walk off with him. He couldn't believe my family had kept me in the dark all this time. No, he had to be toying with me. Like a cat letting the mouse think it had a chance at surviving.

"There wasn't going to be a wedding. Who bought me? Where would those plane tickets really take us? Not Vegas."

"Smarter than I gave you credit for, unless your dear ol' dad told you my plans. You're right. We weren't going to Vegas. Florida. Miami to be exact. A friend has a boat. We were going to hitch a ride until I could make the exchange. You for a shit ton of money." He grinned. "I think I was getting the better deal honestly. You were horrible at sucking cock. Only thing you had going for you was that tight virgin pussy. I'm guessing that's a thing of the past now since you've been shacked up with a biker."

I hate that he made my relationship with Savage seem like something dirty. Compared to his filthy hands, Savage was a damn saint. I'd take that biker over a corrupt cop any day of the week.

"No, I'm not a virgin anymore. And he thinks I suck cock just fine. Can't keep his hands off me."

Ty's eyes narrowed and I realized I may have

gone a bit too far. *Don't poke the bear, especially when he's armed, Mariah.* Ty's hand tightened on the knife, and he advanced two steps closer. "Your original buyer already found another girl, but I'll find someone to take you off my hands. Maybe I'll finally get to fuck you, though. Since you aren't innocent anymore, no harm in sampling the merchandise."

"You're a disgusting pig, Ty. And that's not a slur against cops. Just you. Only a dishonorable, whiny, chickenshit sorry excuse for a man would threaten to rape a woman or sell her to the highest bidder. You're weak. Pathetic. And FYI, your dick is tiny."

"Bitch!" He lunged for me, knife extended like he'd stab me. I forced myself to sit still until the last second, then I dove off the couch and raced to the entry. I didn't know who was outside so I didn't dare leave the house. Not to mention Van and Camille were somewhere nearby. Were they safe?

I ran into the kitchen and snatched up a knife from the sink, thankful I hadn't remembered to finish loading the dishwasher. If that fucker was going to come after me with a knife, then I'd return the favor. And mine was bigger.

He staggered into the kitchen and sneered at me. "What are you going to do, Mariah? Stab me?"

"Maybe. Now it's not just your dick that's tiny. So is your knife." I waved the butcher knife in front of me.

He roared and knocked the chair out of his way before kicking the table over. He came at me, slashing the knife, but I danced out of the way. My heart raced and I hoped like hell he didn't notice I was shaking. I might be acting brave, but I was scared as fuck right now. It wasn't just my life on the line. Where the hell was Savage? Surely someone had figured out Ty was here.

The longer Van stayed gone, the more unsettled I felt. Ty must have hurt him. Was he still alive? And what about Camille? I didn't know if Ty would hesitate to kill a child. He'd been selling underage girls. Men like him probably didn't have too many lines they wouldn't cross.

I had nowhere to run, and no more furniture stood between me and Ty. I might have a bigger knife, but he was twice my size and meaner. No matter how tough I pretended to be, I didn't think I'd win the fight against him. Not on my own. I slipped my hand into my pocket, grasping my phone. Why the hell did nothing have buttons anymore? The older phones could have been dialed without me looking at the damn thing. The smooth screen didn't help me at all.

The second Ty saw the phone in my hand, he'd make his move. He wouldn't give me time to call for help. I'd programmed Savage and Demon as my ICE numbers -- in case of emergency. I hadn't played around with how that would work if I actually needed help. Only one way to find out now. It would either bring Savage home or get me killed faster.

I pulled the phone from my pocket, drawing Ty's attention to it immediately. The second the phone lit up, I pressed the button that would set off my emergency contact chain. For all I knew, it would also contact the police, which could be very bad for the club. I had to take that risk right now, if I was going to get out of this in one piece.

"What the fuck did you just do?" Ty demanded. I set the phone on the kitchen counter and tried to edge closer to the doorway, but he quickly blocked my escape. "Mariah, what did you press on the phone?"

"You'll find out soon enough."

"You bitch! I'm going to have some fun with you. Maybe I'll let your biker watch. Think he'll enjoy seeing another man fuck you?" Ty grinned. "Perhaps I'll leave him alive. Then when I sell you to some cheap brothel south of the border, I can send him video clips of you being used over and over again."

"You're sick, Ty. There's something seriously wrong with you. You get off on that? Hurting women? Watching as other men take a turn?"

He inched closer. "It's even better when they beg for mercy. But the fighters... Mmm. Those are my favorite. Nothing like overpowering a woman and taking what you want."

"You're going to die, Tyson Clarke, and I hope you're tormented every day you're in hell, roasting in the pit. How many women and girls have you sold?"

"Enough. But I'm greedy. There's no such thing as too much money, especially when I haven't been able to spend it the way I want. I was nearly set to walk away from the police department and start my life over on some tropical island far from here. Then you fucked it all up."

"You screwed up, Ty," I said. "You should have never targeted me. Did you really think the Dixie Reapers wouldn't look for me? Don't you know anything about them at all? They take down men like you. Punish them. Make them disappear, and soon, you'll join all the others."

He advanced again, pushing me back to the counter. "You talk a big game, little girl. I don't see your precious biker or your daddy here, do you?"

I caught movement over his shoulder but didn't dare look. Since the person hadn't drawn attention to themselves, I knew help had to have arrived. I just needed to keep Ty distracted.

"I believed you, you know? When you lied and said you loved me. I was ready to marry you, start a life together. All you wanted was to sell me to the highest bidder, but I'd have done anything to make you happy." I tried to relax my body and appear more like the Mariah who'd foolishly loved him. "Anything, Ty. I'd have been yours. Just yours."

He came closer, his grip on the knife loosening a little. It seemed my trick was working. I just needed him to stay focused on me for a few more seconds.

"I loved you," I said. "You told me I'd been horrible at sucking your cock. I'd tried to be good and follow your instructions. I'd wanted to please you, make you feel good. You could have trained me to give you everything you needed. Wouldn't that have been worth more than whatever the man paid for me?"

I could feel the heat of his body as he drew nearer. I'd stroked his ego, and he'd dropped his guard. He reached out to touch my hair, a contemplative look on his face. "It's not too late. You've been used, but if you're a good girl and take your punishment for letting that biker scum touch you, I might take you back. Can you show me you can be a good girl?"

I swallowed back the bile rising up my throat and nodded. "I can. What do you want me to do, Ty? I can make you happy. Let me prove it."

He pointed to the floor. "On your knees, Mariah. You've been his whore the past year. Show me what you've learned. Open up that pretty mouth and suck me off."

I slid down the cabinets until my knees hit the ground. I could see Savage and two others inching into the kitchen, even though I refused to look directly at them. No matter how much I wanted to assure Savage I was playing a part, I couldn't tip my hand. With Ty's back to the doorway, he hadn't seen them.

I tugged at Ty's belt, but my fingers trembled, and I had trouble. I looked up at him, hoping I appeared both frightened and chastened. "I can't, Ty. I'm so worried you won't be pleased with me. I can't get the belt undone. Help me. Please?"

He snorted and closed his knife, shoving it into his pocket. "Not off to a good start, little girl."

I rubbed my hand up and down his thigh. Thankfully, he hadn't noticed I still had my knife. He unbuckled his belt and unfastened his pants. I watched as he tugged the material down a little, then pulled out his cock. I hadn't lied. He really did have a tiny dick. I just hadn't known any better before being with Savage. I'd always thought those porn movies were exaggerated, in all ways. Other than Ty, Savage was the only man I'd seen naked in person.

I leaned forward, my breath ghosting over his skin. I chanced a look up at his face and saw his eyes sliding shut. My grip on the knife tightened and before I could second-guess myself, I jammed it upward, embedding the blade just below the base of his cock.

Ty screamed and stumbled backward, yanking the knife out. It clattered to the floor as he cupped himself, trying to stem the flow of blood. I got to my feet, prepared to run the second I could clear the doorway.

"You fucking cunt! I'm going to make you suffer for this!" He let out a noise that sounded like a scream and ended in a whine. He staggered and looked like his legs might go out from under him at any second.

Savage and Demon both stepped up beside him, eyeing his sorry excuse for a dick. When Savage turned his gaze to me, I had to hold back. I wanted to throw myself into his arms, but not while he stood so close to Ty.

"You okay, baby?" he asked.

I nodded. "Shaken up, but he didn't hurt me. Is he going to bleed out?"

Demon snorted. "From that? No, but I'm sure it hurts like fucking hell. Should have aimed a little higher. Might have taken his dick off."

"Target was too small," I said.

Demon threw back his head and laughed as Savage moved closer to me, a smile curving his lips. He held me against his chest and I finally relaxed, sagging against him. At least I knew the app on my phone worked. Not that I ever wanted to need the damn thing again.

Ty lunged for me, but Demon grabbed him by the back of his shirt and yanked him off his feet. He fell to the floor, cupped his crotch again, and glared at me. If looks could kill, I'd be dead right now. Thankfully I seemed to be tougher than I'd thought.

"Camille and Van!" I tried to pull away from Savage, but he wouldn't let me.

"Stay where you are, baby. They're both fine. Camille was still asleep in her bed. Seems her being deaf was a blessing tonight."

"And Van?" I asked.

"Knocked out. Has a knot the size of a silver dollar on the back of his head, but I think he'll be fine. We'll have the doc check him over. He'll likely have a concussion," Demon said. "We found the window this one used to gain entry and came in the same way."

"There's another man! Someone was pounding on the door when Ty came from the back of the house," I said.

"Got him too." Demon smiled. "You didn't think it was just us, did you?"

"I thought I saw three shadows. When just you and Savage came into the kitchen, I thought I'd been mistaken."

Savage hugged me tighter. "Steel is with Van. Badger, Colorado, and Ripper are babysitting the gorilla who tried to trick you into opening the door. Fucker is huge, but stupid as shit. The second we pinned him, he started talking."

I couldn't help but laugh at his description as I clung to him. I'd been so scared. If he hadn't arrived when he did, I didn't know if I'd have thought to placate Ty. Even stabbing him the way I had apparently wasn't fatal. I'd have just pissed him off more.

"What's going to happen to them?" I asked. I drew back to look up at Savage. "When I used that app, did it notify the police too?"

"Outlaw has it handled. This fucker is ours to do with as we please, same for his friend outside," Savage said. "I can't believe you stabbed him."

"I was worried you'd think I really meant to suck him off. I only wanted to trick him so he'd drop his guard and give you a chance to get into the room, and me a chance to escape. Stabbing him was just a bonus."

Demon kicked Ty in the thigh. "You sell girls and rape women out of rage over having such a tiny dick? We both know it has nothing to do with sex. It's about control and power. You need to feel powerful because someone woman laughed when you dropped your pants?"

"Fuck you!" Ty spat on Demon, which earned him a boot to the face.

Ty sprawled on the kitchen floor, out cold. More

Devil's Fury men came through the front door. Several went to the back of the house while the rest joined us in the kitchen, which was getting overly crowded.

"You want him?" Demon asked Savage.

"As much as I want to rip that asshole apart, I think my woman deserves a shot at vengeance. You done, Mariah? Can the boys have him now?"

"I'm done."

Savage gave Demon a nod. "Take him out of here. Can you get Tal to come clean up the mess and fix that back window?"

"Yeah. Why don't ya'll stay at our place for tonight? Rebel and Camille can bunk together. We'll get the Prospects to scrub this place top to bottom. Erase any traces of Ty and the asshole outside," Demon said.

"Can we?" I asked Savage. "I don't think I can sleep in our room tonight knowing Ty was in there. He contaminated it."

Savage nodded. "Yeah, baby. Go sit in the living room. I'll pack a few things for us and Camille, grab her from her bed, and we can head over there."

"Don't supposed there's a truck so we can drive?" I asked.

"There will be by the time you're ready," Demon said. "I'll call for one. And, Savage, get your family a damn vehicle already. It's not like you can't afford one."

Savage flipped him off as he led me back to the living room. I sank onto the sofa and waited while he gathered our daughter and some clothes. True to his word, Demon had a truck waiting for us when we went outside. I refused to look at the man who'd been beating on the door. I would already have Ty haunting my dreams for a while. I didn't need to add anyone else to the nightmare.

One set of monsters down. One more to go, and then maybe we'd have some peace.

Chapter Twelve

Savage
Two Weeks Later

I looked at the photo in my hand and back at the man on the bench across the street. He didn't look like much. In the videos, when he hurt my daughter and the others, he seemed huge and menacing. As I watched him slumped down, staring at what seemed to be nothing in particular, he looked rather pathetic.

I folded up the photo and shoved it into my pocket before crossing the road. I eased down onto the bench next to him, leaning back and crossing my ankles in front of me. He didn't budge or make a sound. I wasn't entirely certain he even realized someone had joined him.

"You weren't as hard to find as I'd thought you'd be," I said.

He glanced my way, his eyes bloodshot and his skin ashen. "Do I know you?"

"Nope. But you know my daughter, Camille. Had the piece of shit who gave birth to her ever told me of Camille's existence, your filthy hands would have never touched her."

"You here to get revenge for some brat you didn't know about?" he asked.

"I'm here to get vengeance, not just for Camille but for all of them. You're also going to give me a complete list of anyone else like you."

He gave a bark of laughter. "And if I refuse?"

"Oh, I'm sure you will. At first. Don't worry. I can be persuasive. And if you won't listen to me, then I'm sure Camille's mother will make you talk."

He gave me a startled look. "I made sure they killed that bitch."

"At least you admit to sending Destiny off to be slaughtered. I don't give a rat's ass about her. That whore isn't Camille's mother. My wife is rather eager to meet you. I had my reservations, but recent events have proven she can hold her own. If she wants to shed a little blood, I'm not about to stand in her way."

"I won't just walk off with you."

"Didn't think you would." Before he had time to react, Doolittle came up from behind him, sticking a syringe in his neck. The man slumped immediately.

"That should keep him quiet for a while," Doolittle said.

"You didn't have to be here for this," I said. "I know you try not to get your hands too dirty. You're a respectable member of society even if you do wear our colors."

Doolittle shrugged. "He hurts kids for fun, Savage. I can't *not* do anything."

I stood and hefted the man over my shoulder. Doolittle cleared the way to the club truck, laughing about our friend not being able to hold his liquor. Didn't bother me if anyone remembered this asshole being with us. They'd never find him. Unless someone took note of our specific colors, any group of bikers could have nabbed him. As we left town, Doolittle cleared the man's pockets. He popped the SIM card on the phone and tossed it out the window. The phone went into a trash can at the first gas station we found.

This man was mine to do with as I pleased. The others were another matter. I'd let Outlaw and the other hackers send the files they'd been compiling on the ones we already knew about. Any new names would be researched and the same would happen. I didn't have a problem with the Feds stepping in and taking out the rest of the trash. But this one right here... only place he was going was six feet under.

By the time we pulled into the compound, it was getting dark. I pulled to the back of our property and carried the man into the trees. No one could see us from here, and if anyone flew a drone over the property, the canopy would hide our actions. Since those damn things had become popular for anyone to pick up at the store, we'd had to exercise a bit more caution even on our own land. Technology could be a pain in my ass sometimes. Other times, like when Mariah sent that alert out, I was grateful.

"You staying?" I asked Doolittle, thinking we'd part ways about now. Injecting the man with a sedative was one thing. What I had planned was another matter.

"I'm not going anywhere. Demon is bringing Mariah, right?"

"Yeah. At least that's what he said. Camille will be staying the night at his house. Farrah and Rebel will keep her occupied."

I heard a few bikes pulling up and looked over to see my woman on the back of Van's bike. I folded my arms and stared her down. Not only did she know I didn't want her riding on a fucking motorcycle while she was pregnant, but she wasn't permitted on the back of any bike other than mine and possibly her dad's. I'd be spanking her ass for sure later.

"Woman, get your ass off that bike!" I yelled.

She narrowed her eyes but got off and walked over to me. "It wasn't like you came to pick me up, and you haven't bought me a car yet. You've had ample opportunity, and even your club has brought it up. What did you want me to do? Walk?"

I growled, hating that she was right. *Fuck!* "Fine. You get a pass just this once. You're riding back with me in the truck."

She eyed the man on the ground. "That him?"

"Yep. Should be waking up shortly. Right, Doolittle?" I asked.

"Yeah. Unless I gave him too much. I didn't exactly have his medical chart to consult for height and weight. I had to guess. Plus, I'm used to treating the furry types of animals, not the human variety."

Mariah patted his back. "I think you just insulted animals everywhere by lumping him in with them."

He smiled. "You're right."

The man on the ground groaned and started to move. I nodded at Demon who drove four stakes into the ground and wound ropes around them. While he took care of that task, Ripper removed the man's clothes and shoes. Once he'd been stripped bare, Demon tied him down. He'd just secured the last knot when the asshole jolted fully awake.

"Where am I? Let me go!" He struggled but couldn't break free.

"Let me introduce you to someone. My wife. Camille's mother. I think she'd like to have a few words with you." I let Mariah move in closer. It wasn't like the man could hurt her. Hell, even if he wasn't tied down, she could probably still handle him.

She held out her hand and I knew what she wanted. I pulled the knife from my belt and let her have it. Mariah dropped to her knees next to the man and stared at him. When her gaze slid down to his cock, she growled.

"I know what you did to Camille. Do you know how it makes me feel to know she was scared? You hurt her, terrorized her, and enjoyed every second, didn't you?" she asked. The man refused to answer. Big mistake. I knew Mariah wouldn't take too kindly to being ignored. She leaned in closer, bracing her weight, and the knife, against his upper thigh. "Does hurting little girls make you feel like a big man? You get off on touching them and making them touch you?"

He turned his face away. Mariah hissed at him like a pissed-off kitten and dragged the blade of the knife along his inner thigh. He screamed and thrashed, causing her to nick his ball sac.

"What's his name?" she asked, looking over at me.

"No names, baby. He isn't worthy of having anyone here use his name. Just call him asshole, or pedophile. Either one works. Pretty soon we'll be calling him dead."

She tapped his dick with the flat of the blade and I tried not to wince. "Did this part of him touch Camille? You never told me exactly what she went through, and I didn't want to know. But now... You said there was a reason she didn't like her mouth touched, and I'm not sure I like the conclusion I'm drawing."

I hesitated and it was the only confirmation she needed. I didn't even get a chance to react before she grabbed his cock and cut it off. Every fucking brother took a step back, wincing as they cupped themselves -- including me -- as she waved it front of his face. The man reacted immediately, the sounds coming from him sounding inhuman. I expected him to pass out any second. "Doesn't look too impressive to me. Guess you won't be using it to hurt children anymore."

"Jesus," Demon muttered. "And I thought my woman was a damn psycho. I think yours just trumped her."

"So..." Van rocked back on his heels. "The rest of us aren't needed, are we? Won't be long before he bleeds out."

"Mariah, sweetheart, did you have to take all the fun away from everyone? I kind of wanted to defend my daughter."

She stood and held out her hand, dropping the knife. "I need about three gallons of hand sanitizer, and then some boiling water and anti-bacterial soap to get his germs off me. I can't believe I touched his dick."

She shivered. I kissed her forehead and handed her off to Wolf. "Stay here. The rest of us need to work fast if we want him to suffer more before he dies."

Van, Demon, and Doolittle all stepped in. We each took a limb and sawed through them. The shithead passed out before we'd gotten very far, and I felt cheated. Mariah was right though. He wouldn't hurt anyone ever again. As I hacked through another chunk of his leg, I heard retching and turned to see Mariah throwing up a few feet away.

"You can cut off his dick, but you can't handle this?" I asked.

She waved me off. "Carry on. Don't mind me."

Wolf held her hair back while she finished purging her stomach. I should have insisted she remain with Camille, but I had a feeling she'd have found a way to get here on her own. Or talked someone into bringing her.

I stepped back and let my brothers bag up the body. The pieces would be scattered and buried. I hadn't thought about driving the truck back home while covered in blood. Couldn't be helped. Mariah let Wolf guide her over to the truck and help her onto the seat. After he shut the door, I got behind the wheel and headed to the house.

"Sorry about that," she said.

"Which part? You cutting off his dick right away

so he bled out too fast? Or puking?"

She shrugged. "Both."

I shook my head but couldn't help smiling a little. "Baby girl, I love that you wanted to get back at him for what he did to Camille, but I had plans for him. I'd wanted him to suffer more, and I'd also hoped to get more names out of him. We'll have to hope there aren't more men like him we didn't track down."

"I didn't even think about that." She tipped her head back and closed her eyes. "I fucked up, but I was so angry."

"We'll go home and get cleaned up. Demon said Camille could stay at his house all night. They'll take care of her and bring her back sometime tomorrow. Think you and I could use a night alone."

She cracked an eye open and looked at me. "We're both covered in the blood of a pedophile and you're over there thinking about having sex?"

"No. Not exactly." I shifted in the seat. "I'm covered in his blood and thinking about washing it off, with you, in the shower. Which made me think about you naked and covered in soap, and... Yeah. I detoured to sex from there."

"You're incorrigible."

"It's part of what you love about me." I winked at her, loving it when her cheeks flushed. We hadn't said the words to one another, but I could tell her feelings for me ran just as deep as mine did for her.

I stopped the truck in our driveaway. I did have one bit of good news I could share with Mariah. I'd thought to wait until Camille was with us in the morning, but... she looked like she could use a bit of cheer right now.

"The doctor called," I said.

"Which one?"

"The auditory specialist we took Camille to last week. He thinks she may benefit from a cochlear implant. He said he'd send some information to the house and we could decide what we wanted to do. There's a chance Camille could hear, Mariah. Our little girl could hear our voices, amongst other things."

Tears gathered in her eyes. "Really?"

I nodded. "But it's a big decision. There are some risks involved. Once we get the packet in the mail, we can look it over and talk about it some more."

"Can we go shower now? I feel icky."

"All right, baby. Sit tight. I'm coming around to get you."

I got out of the truck and went around to get her. Since we both had blood on us, I didn't see the harm in carrying her into the house. I walked straight through to the bathroom. After I set her on the counter, I started the shower, then helped her remove her clothes.

Before things went any further, there was one thing I still needed to do. She'd ridden with another man, one not related to her, and I couldn't let it stand. I sat on the side of the tub and crooked a finger at her.

"What?" she asked.

"Over my lap, baby. You knew better than to ride with Van. Now you get a spanking."

I saw her clench her thighs together. I reached out a hand and she took it, letting out a shaky breath. Once she'd settled over my thighs, I ran my palm over her ass cheeks. Seeing her like this, so trusting and vulnerable, did something to me.

"I think you've earned six spankings. Count them out," I said.

I brought my hand down, making sure the first swat wasn't too hard.

"One," she said, sounding breathy.

I cracked my hand against her ass twice more in rapid succession, a little harder.

"Two. Three."

Smack.

"Four."

I didn't hold back on the last two. Her ass would be red, but maybe she'd remember not to get on the back of another man's bike.

Smack. Smack.

She squeaked and tensed. "Five. Six."

I could feel the heat coming off her fair skin and admired my handiwork before letting her up. She stood and rubbed at her ass, wincing.

"Wasn't supposed to tickle, sweetheart. You going to ride on the back of Van's bike again? Or anyone's but mine?"

"Not without permission," she mumbled.

I smiled and let Mariah get in first while I stripped down before joining her.

Mariah shampooed her hair, and I started washing. I admired her curves and couldn't wait to get my hands on her. Was she right? Was I a little fucked up? Yeah, we'd just killed a man, if you could call him that. I wasn't sure someone so evil deserved to be labeled as human. Perhaps living the life I had over the last two decades and some change had skewed my moral compass. Just a little.

Far as I was concerned, we'd just done the world a great service. No reason not to revel however we saw fit. And right now, I wanted to celebrate by being balls-deep in my sexy woman. I finished cleaning myself, then helped Mariah rinse. The last of the soap slid down her body and I pressed her back against the tiled wall.

"Not even going to take me to the bed?" she

asked, a teasing glint in her eyes.

"I will. Later."

She put her hands on my shoulders and slid her foot up my calf. I took advantage and gripped her hips, lifting her off the ground. Her legs went around my waist, and I rocked against her, letting my cock slide along the lips of her pussy.

"That's not just water slicking your skin, is it?" I asked.

She shook her head. "I got all hot and bothered while you were washing. Seeing your hand slide up and down your cock was like watching a live porno."

"Just what do you know about porn?"

She leaned in closer and whispered, "More than you think. Now fuck me, Gates. I need you inside me."

I eased inside her, taking my time. I loved how she squirmed and pressed her heels against me, trying to make me move faster. I sank fully into her and savored the moment. Mariah always felt like perfection. Hot. Wet. So fucking tight.

I kissed her as I stroked in and out of her. "Love you, Mariah."

She jerked her gaze to mine, looking like a startled deer. "You do?"

"Think I've loved you since the beginning. You and Camille are everything to me. And the little one we haven't met yet. I love your strength. Your courage. These sexy curves are a bonus. I'm a lucky bastard, Mariah, because you're mine."

She cupped my cheek as I stilled, buried inside her. "I love you too, Gates. More than you'll ever know."

I pressed my lips to hers before pulling out and spinning her to face the wall. I yanked her hips back and plunged inside her, fucking her hard and deep.

My hips slapped against her ass as I drove into her, until I felt her pussy clench down and the gush of her release. She cried out my name and I lost control. The primitive part of me took over and I slammed into her over and over until I came, filling her up with my cum. Even then I didn't slow. My cock stayed hard long enough for me to wring another three orgasms from her.

When I pulled out, I watched our mingled release slide down the inside of her thigh. My cock still pointed up, and I had a feeling it was going to be a long night. I'd thought I didn't need those words but hearing her say she loved me was like a fucking aphrodisiac.

"Better clean you up again, baby. So I can get you dirty all over again."

She smiled at me over her shoulder, and I knew she wouldn't complain. She was my perfect match. Not only did she crave my touch as much as I craved hers, but she was a wildcat in the bedroom, and a feisty kitten the rest of the time. I adored everything about her.

Twenty years with her wouldn't be enough. Forty wouldn't be either. I wanted a lifetime and more with this incredible woman by my side, and I'd do whatever it took to ensure we could spend as long as possible together. Even if it meant disposing of more evil men along the way.

Epilogue

"Savage!" Mariah yelled across the house. "Why the hell is the banana pudding gone?"

I entered the kitchen, hiding a spoon behind my back and trying not to look guilty as fuck. "What banana pudding?"

She folded her arms. "The one I made to take over to Farrah and Demon's house today for the picnic. The entire dish is missing from the fridge."

"Um." I felt my cheeks flush. "I got hungry."

My woman rolled her eyes and walked out to our newly finished garage. She came back with another banana pudding in her hands, which meant she'd hid it in the overflow fridge we kept out there. "Don't touch this one!"

"Yes, ma'am." I winked. "But can you make more pudding later? I can think of a few fun ways to eat it while the girls are visiting their grandparents later."

"Oh, yeah?"

I moved closer and tossed the spoon into the sink before caging her against the counter. "I'd like to lick it off your pretty nipples. Maybe suck it off your clit."

Her thighs clenched and her cheeks turned a rosy pink. "Gates! The girls are…"

"Busy. They're packing everything they can cram into their suitcases even though they're just staying overnight. Now be a good girl, Mariah. Unbutton your dress."

Her breath caught as she reached for the small buttons down her bodice. She unfastened them and the material gaped open, exposing the swells of her breasts. They'd stayed large even after she'd given birth and stopped breastfeeding, and I fucking loved them. "Show me your nipples. I bet they're hard, aren't they? You turned-on, baby girl?"

"You know I am," she said softly. She tugged the cups of her bra down and I groaned at how beautiful she was. I lifted the hem of her dress and tugged on her panties.

"Step out of these and wrap your legs around me."

She obeyed and I easily thrust inside her. Her breasts bounced with every stroke, making me harder than steel. I knew we didn't have much time, so it was going to be quick. Reaching between us, I rubbed her clit and placed my lips against hers when she started to get loud. I kissed her as I came inside her. My cock twitched even after the last drop of cum had left my balls, and I knew if we had more time, I'd be bending her over the table and taking her again.

I pumped into her a few more times, loving the way her pussy clasped me. I felt her nails biting in my shoulders and knew she was already close again. I kept fucking her until she'd come one more time. "I wish I could stay inside you longer." I ground against her. "Tonight, you're all mine."

"Ever since the doctor gave the all clear for us to have sex again, you've been insatiable."

"I'm only getting started, Mariah. I love Camille and Iris, but I think they need a little brother."

Her eyes went wide. "Savage! I just gave birth a few months ago. You're already trying to knock me up again?"

"Nope. I'm just going to fuck you every chance I get. If we happen to make another baby..." I shrugged a shoulder and grinned at her.

"All right, you heathen. Put me down and give me my panties back. We need to get over to Farrah's. Then I'm all yours when we come back home tonight. Just behave in front of my parents, please."

I kissed her once more, as I pulled out. "I make no promises. And you don't get your panties back. I want you bare."

She pushed at my chest. "I'm not going to see my parents while I'm not wearing anything under my dress!"

"Good idea. Take the bra off too." I grinned when she mock-punched me in the arm. The way she blushed told me she liked my idea. I had a feeling she'd be going without undies today, which meant first chance I got, I'd be bending her over the bathroom sink or taking her up against a wall.

It had been two years since I'd agreed to make Mariah mine. I'd hoped we would grow to care for one another, and I'd looked forward to spending my life with someone. It never occurred to me I'd want her more than I'd ever wanted another woman, or that I'd come to love her so damn much.

She'd just gotten her dress put back into place when Camille came racing around the corner, pushing Iris in a stroller. I'd learned the hard way not to shout or Camille would accidentally dump the baby over. Even though I hated when she ran with her sister, it was safer to not react. Our eldest daughter liked helping with her baby sister. Since Camille wasn't big enough to carry Iris, we kept a stroller in the house.

"You ready to see your grandparents?" I asked my girls. Iris just blinked at me, but Camille bounced up and down.

We'd gotten her cochlear implant six months ago, and while her hearing would never be perfect at least she could talk to us now. We still used sign language when we could, but it wasn't necessary anymore.

I wrapped my arm around Mariah and smiled down at Camille and Iris. My girls. My family. "Love you three," I said.

"Love you, Daddy," Camille said in her sing-song voice. My heart warmed every time I heard those words.

One day a couple of assholes would come along and try to take my girls for their own. I hoped they were ready for a fight, because I damn sure wasn't going to let them walk off with just anyone. Especially not a horny bastard like their dad. Nope, my little angels would remain pure until I found just the right men for them, and fuck anyone who tried to say otherwise. There was too much evil in the world for me to entrust them to just anyone.

"You're looking a little homicidal," Mariah whispered. "Stop thinking about them growing up and moving out. Otherwise *I'll* be punishing *you*."

"Oh, yeah?"

She nodded. "Yep. No sex for a week."

Well, damn. The woman knew how to hit me where it hurt most. Looked like I'd have to be on my best behavior... until I could distract her. I lowered my hand to her ass and gave it a squeeze, earning me a sharp glare, but I saw the flare of heat in her eyes. Yeah, she wanted me just as much as I wanted her. I had a feeling this would be a quick trip today, then we'd have all night without the girls.

"We have the house to ourselves tonight," I whispered. "Consider the possibilities."

She smiled and turned away to pick up the banana pudding from the counter. I followed her out of the house with Camille pushing Iris in the stroller.

I'd turned in my bad-boy card and taken on the role of daddy and husband, even if Mariah and I hadn't officially gotten married. One day. For now, what we had worked for us. As long as I got to call her mine, that's all that mattered.

Against the Wall (A Bad Boy Romance)
Harley Wylde

Wanted: One hunky handyman to mend her lonely heart.

Grady: Handyman and heartbreaker. I'm damn good at my job. While my hands have been occupied building a deck for the delectable Madelyn Sparks, what I've really wanted to do is trace every one of her curves with my tongue. I bet with just one touch she'd go up in flames. My dick's been harder than a damn post since I took this job, but I learned the hard way not to fuck myself out of a paycheck. But once this job is done, all bets are off.

Madelyn: Grady has done a fantastic job on the deck, but I didn't really hire him for his carpentry skills. The man is fine as hell and I've wanted to take him for a ride ever since I saw him on my doorstep. Never in my wildest dreams did I think getting attacked would bring us closer together. He went from hunky handyman to overprotective bodyguard in an instant, and now that we're living under the same roof, I just can't keep my hands off him. Just one problem... now that I've had him, I never want to let him go.

Chapter One

Grady

The sound of my drill was loud in the otherwise quiet backyard. I'd been working on this massive deck for two days for a pampered princess, but there were perks aside from a paycheck. I glanced toward the lounger by the pool and couldn't help but admire the tanned perfection of Madelyn Sparks. She might be petite, but she was all legs and curves. Definitely a mouthwatering package.

The sun beat down on me and sweat rolled down my temples to drip off my chin onto the wooden deck below. I'd literally put my blood and sweat into the thing, but tears weren't going to happen. Not unless the goddess decided to kick me in the nuts for staring too much. She did a pretty good job of ignoring me, even when I drooled. Couldn't really blame her. A guy like me was too far beneath someone like her. The house she lived in had to cost at least half a million, if not more. My bungalow was a little too damn close to the questionable part of town and probably could have fit in her garage.

I put in one last screw and wiped my brow before standing. My back cracked as I stretched and put the tools away. As much as I would have loved to stare at perfection a little while longer, it was time to call it a day. I had an ice cold shower waiting for me at home, along with a beer and a bag of pretzels. The dinner of champions. Or rather, the dinner of a broke handyman. This job was going to pay really damn well, but I didn't get the check until I finished the deck.

The scent of suntan oil reached my nose, and I turned to see Little Miss Perfect. She pushed her sunglasses on top of her honey blonde tresses and smiled at me.

"Finished for the day?" she asked.

"Yeah, I thought I'd pack it up and come back first thing tomorrow. Eight o'clock okay?"

Her nose wrinkled a little. "As long as you don't mind me being crabby. I don't finish my morning coffee until nine."

I couldn't help but smile at her. Something told me that even at her crabbiest she was damn cute. She couldn't have been more than twenty-one or twenty-two. I felt ancient at close to thirty, even though there were only a handful of years between us. I put my tools by the back gate and waited to see if she would say or do anything else.

"Would you like some water or soda to take with you?" she asked. "I even have some of that flavored stuff you can add to a bottle of water."

I must have made a face because she laughed and crooked a finger at me. Like a little lost puppy, I trailed after her and into the pristine house, my boots clunking along the hardwood floors. Her kitchen was huge, with spotless granite countertops and stainless steel appliances.

"Nice place," I commented as I took in my surroundings. I'd never own a place like this. Not because I didn't want one, but because I wasn't going to earn enough ever to climb this high up the social ladder.

"It was my parents' home. They died last year and left everything to me."

Well, that explained why she was so rich at such a young age, but it had to suck to lose her family like that. My mom was still very much alive and living it up in Vegas as a retired showgirl. I'd never known my dad, and I wasn't sure Mom had ever known who he was. Just some nameless man who had crossed paths with her at some point. Along with countless others. Mom hadn't exactly been known for being a one-man woman back in the day. Or now, for that matter.

"I'm sorry for your loss," I told her.

She gave me a small smile and opened the fridge. "Water or soda? I have a beer, but I doubt it's one you'd like to drink. I've been told it's a girly beer."

I laughed and told her water was fine. It was the best way to stay hydrated in this horrible heat. I guzzled half the bottle before I even took a breath. Madelyn had her hip propped against the counter, and her gaze traveled over me. I couldn't help but grow hard under her perusal. If she noticed, she was good at pretending otherwise. There was heat in her eyes as she looked up at me. Part of me hoped for the green light to kiss her the way I'd wanted to since the moment she opened her front door several days ago. The other part worried I'd screw myself out of a paycheck again and told me to keep it in my pants.

I finished my water and tossed the bottle into the trashcan. As much as I wanted to linger, I couldn't think of a reason not to leave. My work for the day was done, and she wasn't exactly saying much to keep me in her house. Then again, I was sweating all over her pristine floors. She probably couldn't wait for me to leave.

"Thanks for the water," I told her. "I'll see you tomorrow at eight."

"Let me walk you out."

"That's okay. I'll just go out the back way. I left my tools by the back gate."

She nodded, and if I wasn't mistaken, there was a hint of sadness in her eyes as I turned to walk away. I wondered if maybe she was a little lonely, living in

such a big place all by herself. For all I knew, she had a
string of men waiting at her beck and call, but I hadn't
seen a single person any of the days I'd been here.

Her gaze drilled into my back as I made my way
through her house to the back door. The humid air
smacked me in the face as I stepped outside and made
my way over to the gate. I picked up my tools and let
myself out of the backyard. My truck was parked at the
curb. I hadn't wanted to take a chance on the damn
thing leaking oil on her driveway. I shoved my stuff
into the backseat and climbed in. As I was about to pull
away, a flashy car pulled into her driveway, and a guy
in a pink polo and khakis got out. Figured she'd go for
a sissy boy like that one. His build was slight, and the
softer angles of his face made him almost appear
feminine. If he had any muscle on him, it definitely
came from a gym. Guys like that didn't get their hands
dirty.

With a shake of my head, I pulled away and
drove home to the other side of town. Living in a small
town meant it didn't take long to reach the house. My
driveway was cracked and uneven and my porch
drooped, but it was home sweet home. I killed the
engine and got out, taking my tools with me. No way I
would leave them in the truck in this neighborhood.
Not unless I wanted them stolen. After I unlocked the
door and pushed it open, I stepped inside and
immediately frowned. It felt like it was a million
degrees in the house.

The air conditioner in the front window still
hummed, but when I stepped closer and held out my
hand, only hot air came out of it. I'd just cleaned the
thing the week before, so I knew that wasn't it. It
looked like the four-year-old unit had finally called it
quits. As I walked through the house, I noticed the

other even older units were not on or were sending out blasts of hot air as well. Just what I needed, the cost of four window units. Hell, even the cost of one was too much. There was only twenty bucks in my account until I got paid for my current job either tomorrow or day after, depending on how long it took me to wrap things up.

I went into the bedroom and turned on the ceiling fan before stripping out of my clothes. In the bathroom, I turned on the shower and didn't even bother with the hot water. An icy stream hit me straight in the face as I stepped under the spray and it helped cool my heated skin. I stayed in the shower as long as I could, knowing I would just be miserable once I got out. After I dried off and pulled on a pair of boxer briefs, I contemplated what the hell I was going to do the rest of the night. In this neighborhood leaving a window open was just asking for trouble, so that was out.

As I tried to figure out what to do, my phone started ringing. I frowned when I saw the number on the display. What the hell was the princess calling me about? Had I left something at her place? I accepted the call and put the phone up to my ear. Before I could even say hello, I heard her sobbing on the other end.

"Madelyn? What's wrong?"

She cried even harder. "I... need... you."

"You need me? What happened?"

"Please come."

I didn't get a chance to say another word before she disconnected the call. A bad feeling came over me as I threw on a fresh pair of jeans and a tee. I doubted she was crying over her deck, so I passed up my work boots for a pair of tennis shoes. It only took me a moment to dig my wallet and keys out of my discarded clothes, and I ran for the door, stopping only long enough to lock the place up. Breaking every speed limit in town, I screeched to a halt at her curb about ten minutes later.

I rang her doorbell and waited. When she didn't answer, I banged on it with my fist, hoping I wouldn't shatter the pretty stained glass. Still no Madelyn. I hesitated only a moment before I reached for the knob and let myself in. I heard sniffles and crying coming from the back of the house. When I entered the kitchen, she was curled into a corner near the stove with her phone clutched in her hand and her head hanging down, hair obscuring her face.

Kneeling in front of her, I slowly reached out and tipped her chin up. I couldn't stop the curse that fell from my lips when I took in her bruised cheek and split lip.

"What the hell did that bastard do to you?" I asked with a growl to my tone.

"He wouldn't take no for an answer."

My heart kicked in my chest, and I looked her over, but her clothing didn't seem to be in disarray. I hoped like hell when she said he wouldn't take no for an answer that it hadn't meant he'd raped her. I gently scooped her into my arms and carried her into the living room. The waning sunlight filtered through the floor to ceiling windows, but I flicked on the lamp to get a better look at her.

"Do you have an ice pack?" I asked, thinking we needed to get the swelling down in her lip and cheek.

"Freezer."

I left her long enough to see what she had available. There were two gel ice packs in the freezer door, and I pulled both out, carrying them back to her. I placed one against her cheek and motioned for her to put the other against her lip.

"You need to call the police."

She shook her head. "You don't understand. His daddy is a state senator, and his uncle is the mayor. The police aren't going to do anything but laugh at me."

"You need a restraining order, Madelyn. You can't let him get away with this."

"They won't do anything," she insisted.

"Then they'll waste their time coming out here because I'm calling them."

I pulled my cell phone from my pocket and dialed 9-1-1. After assuring the operator the guy wasn't on the premises anymore and answering all of her questions, I sat and waited for the dispatched units to arrive. After fifteen minutes, I could hear sirens in the distance and hoped that was them. I thanked the operator and hung up, taking Madelyn's hand on mine.

"I'm going to go wait for them on the porch."

She shook her head and held onto me tighter. "Don't leave me."

"Why did you call me?" I asked, having to know why me and not one of her rich friends. It wasn't like we were close, even if I had spent the last few days drooling over her while I worked.

"You make me feel safe," she said. "I knew you wouldn't let him hurt me anymore."

Pride swelled inside at her words, and she was damn right. I wasn't about to let anything else happen to her, not if I could help it. If the asshole was as connected as she said, then I knew it would be an uphill battle, but I'd stand by her while she figured things out. Hopefully, the police would listen and actually take the damn report and not brush her off.

When the officers knocked on the door, I yelled for them to come in and told them our location, and as an afterthought, I added that neither of us was armed. A paramedic was on their heels, and I was grateful someone would be able to take a look at Madelyn in case she needed more than ice to heal her. She looked pretty rough.

I tried to get out of the way, but she held tight to my hand when the officers began questioning her.

"And who are you?" the older officer asked.

"He's my friend, Grady O'Bryan," Madelyn said. "I called him when Bradley left. I didn't know what else to do."

"And that's Bradley Simon?" the second officer asked, as he took notes.

Madelyn nodded.

"I know he's supposed to be related to the mayor, but you're going to do something to stop him from coming back, aren't you?" I asked.

The officers shared a look, and I knew it meant trouble.

"Do you want to file a restraining order?" the younger officer asked. "You can come down to the station and fill out the proper forms, and we can get the ball rolling. With it just being your word against his, we can't really arrest him. Unless there was a witness?"

Madelyn shook her head.

The older man looked at me. "What do you know about Bradley Simon?"

"Nothing. Madelyn told me he's connected to the mayor and a state senator, but that's as much as I know about the guy. Is there something we should be aware of?"

The officer rested his hands on his belt. "This

doesn't leave this room, but I can't stand a guy who abuses women. Mr. Simon has a series of complaints against him that all magically go away before making it to court. All charges are always dropped, or the women disappear. He's a known abuser and has even been accused of rape."

My stomach soured at the picture they painted.

"If I were you, I'd get her out of here. And I don't just mean on vacation. She needs to start over somewhere he can't find her, preferably a large city, because once he sets his sights on someone, he doesn't back down until he gets what he wants." The officer looked disgusted. "I'd arrest his ass and throw him in jail, but my chief would have my ass. He plays golf with the mayor every Saturday. The judge is a family friend too, so I doubt the charges would stick."

Great. Madelyn looked a little defeated, and I didn't know what to say or do to help her. With my dwindling bank account, I wasn't in a position to help her escape. Even if she asked me to go with her, it wasn't like I could just pack up and leave. Could I? My house wasn't much, but I did own the damn thing. I had roots in this town.

She lifted her face and gazed at me with tears in her eyes. And I knew, I was going to do whatever it damn well took to keep her safe.

Even if it fucked me over.

I always had been a sucker for a damsel in distress. It seemed my princess needed my help. Her lower lip trembled, so I squeezed her hand, letting her know that I was with her, whatever happened next. I couldn't leave her on her own, not knowing that bastard might come back. He was a twisted fuck, and if I left her to his mercy, I'd be just as guilty of whatever crime he committed against her.

Fuck.

Every time life handed me lemons, all I got was sour ass lemon juice.

Chapter Two

Madelyn

When the officers left, I was shaking. I'd known that Bradley was bad news, but I hadn't realized just how bad. Now that I was catching a glimpse of the monster inside, I had no doubt he'd either gotten rid of those women himself or paid someone to do it. And how likely was it that his dad didn't know what was going on, or his uncle for that matter? It sickened me, the lengths they would go to cover up a crime, just so their precious name wasn't smeared in the papers.

Poor Grady hadn't signed on for this. The man had only won the bid to build my deck, and while that might have had more to do with his good looks than his price, I still couldn't ask him to help me hide out while I figured out what to do. My parents hadn't been without connections, even though I'd never called on any of them for favors in the past. No one knew just how well-connected my mother had been, and I wanted to keep it that way for a little while longer.

"I can't ask you to help me," I told him, licking my sore lip. "You have a life here, a business to run."

He snorted. "I have about twenty bucks in the bank, so we're not getting far if I help you."

"I have money. More than I know what to do with, quite honestly. It still doesn't give me the right to uproot your life. You've done enough for me already just by being here tonight. I can't thank you enough for coming to my rescue."

Grady knelt by my feet and took my hand in his. "Madelyn, I'm glad you called me. You shouldn't have tried facing this alone. Honestly, though, I can't figure out why you called me instead of one of your friends. We were complete strangers until a few days ago."

How could I put this delicately? My friends were upper crust yuppies with trust funds and no self-defense skills. Grady looked like he could handle himself in a fight, with all those muscles and that swagger. Bradley might have taken me down, and he could probably take down any of my friends, but I knew there was no way in hell he'd try to tangle with Grady. He'd have to be stupid to attempt it.

"My friends are on the light side," I said.

"You mean they're gay? Because I've met some gay men who could knock me out with one punch."

"Well, some of them are gay, but I mean more like…" I sighed. "I'm just going to give it to you straight. My guy friends might weigh 150 pounds soaking wet and would blow over with a stiff wind. Bradley wasn't going to be run off by any of them. But you… you're like a walking mountain with all those muscles. I figured if he came back, one look at you and he'd go running the other way. I knew if it came down to it, you could protect me."

Grady smiled a little, and the knots in my stomach eased. I'd worried that I would offend him. He really did make me feel safe, though, and it wasn't just his muscles. It was the confidence he exuded, the predatory look in his eyes that said he'd seen more shit than most, and I just felt calm when I was around him. I was normally a very nervous and twitchy person, but not when Grady was nearby.

"Do you know how to use a gun?" I asked.

His eyebrows rose as he stared at me. "Why do I need to know how to use a gun? If you want me to hunt down Bradley and shoot him, I'm afraid you'll have to find someone else. I prefer life on this side of the bars."

"No, no. Nothing like that." I bit my lip then

winced when it stung. "I obviously need protection until I can get the Bradley situation taken care of. And I know I still owe you for the deck you're building for me, which looks fantastic by the way."

"Get to the point, princess."

Princess? Is that how he saw me? Some pampered poodle? In all fairness, it wasn't far off.

"Have you ever done any work as a bodyguard?" I asked.

"Not exactly."

Not exactly didn't mean no. "Okay, so maybe not a bodyguard, but you've done some kind of protection work before, right?"

"I was a Marine for five years. Joined up right out of high school, served my five years and got out. Being sent to a war zone isn't my idea of a good time. I'm proud to have served, but five years was enough."

My gaze took him in from head to toe. Yeah, I could see him as a Marine. And damn if that didn't just make him even sexier. I'd always had a thing for men in uniform. I wondered if he still wore his dog tags, or if he'd hung them up when he'd decided to live life as a civilian.

"If I pay you an additional two thousand dollars, would you consider being my bodyguard for the next week? Just long enough for me to figure out what the heck I'm going to do. You could still work on the deck while you're here if you're worried about being free to work on other jobs afterward."

"Bodyguard?"

"I'd need you to stay here though. Overnight, I mean. And you'd have to go with me if I left the house."

He looked like he was thinking it over, but I was worried he'd tell me no. I needed him. Yes, I could hire a security firm, but I wanted Grady. Perhaps it had a little to do with the fact I wanted to spend more time with him. There had to be a way I could tempt him.

"Three thousand," I offered. "And two of my friends need some work done on their houses, so I could refer you."

Although, the thought of Jenna watching Grady work up a sweat made me want to growl in protest. For some reason, I thought of him as mine. Ridiculous, since we barely knew one another. He stared at me, and I wondered if I needed to up the price again. It wasn't like I couldn't afford to pay him more.

"I would have done it for less, Madelyn. I just think if you're serious about protection, you should probably hire a professional."

"So, you'd rather trust my safety to someone who took some sort of class to be an armed guard instead of a Marine?"

He smiled a little. "If you're serious, I'll need to go to my place and get some clothes. I can't go a week with just the clothes on my back, but my neighborhood isn't the safest."

"We could go shopping," I offered. "My treat. Consider it part of your pay."

"I don't need new clothes, Madelyn. The ones I have are just fine."

"I didn't mean to imply they weren't, but I just thought if I can't go to your place then I'd just buy you some new things."

He shook his head and ran a hand through his hair. "We'll go to my place, but I have to warn you... the air is out. You're going to melt the moment you walk through the door."

"I think I'll survive."

"All right, princess. If we're going to do this, let's

get it out of the way. Then we'll figure out sleeping arrangements when we get back."

Sleeping arrangements? Would now be a good time to offer up my bed -- with me in it? He was a red-blooded man, so I didn't think he'd turn me down. Unless he was one of those honorable types who wouldn't want to take advantage of me. Since he hadn't made a move in the three days he'd been here, I had a feeling he was one of those rare men who put others before himself. I'd caught a heated look or two, so I knew he wanted me. But would he allow himself to have me? Only time would tell.

I looked down at my swimsuit and shorts. "Do I have time to change?"

"Trust me; you'll be thankful you're not wearing much. I wasn't kidding when I said the air was out. Afghanistan feels like the arctic compared to my house right now."

"Then let's go get your stuff. When we get back, I'll order some takeout for us. Chinese sound good? Or I could call that takeout delivery service that just started up. I think they deliver from five different restaurants."

"Chinese is fine," he said.

I rose to my feet, even though I felt a little unsteady. "I'm ready. Do you want to take my car?"

He shook his head. "Better to take my truck. Taking your car would just be asking for trouble. It would probably get stolen."

Just where did he live? I hadn't ventured to the other side of town before, the area my dad had always called the "wrong" side. I followed him out to his truck and Grady helped me up onto the seat. The drive to his house was quiet, but I noticed his grip on the steering wheel was pretty tight. Was he nervous about me seeing where he lived? I didn't care if he lived in the smallest dump in town or the biggest mansion. Stuff like that had never mattered to me.

He pulled to a stop in front of a small bungalow, and I had to admit it was in pretty sad shape. It seemed odd for a handyman to live in a place that had fallen into disrepair, but he probably spent so much time working, he didn't want to work on his own place after hours. I couldn't fault him for that. We got out of the truck, and he looked around as he guided me up the porch steps. When he pushed open the front door, the blast of heat that came out of his house made me glad I'd asked him to stay with me. No one should have to suffer in these high temps without air.

He led me through the house to his bedroom. The unmade bed was small for a guy his size, and his furniture looked secondhand. Despite the shabbiness of everything, I had to admit the place was pretty clean. The clothes he'd worn earlier were discarded on the floor, but aside from that, the place was spotless. He threw some things into a duffle bag and grabbed his work boots before motioning for me to head back to the front door.

Grady locked up, tossed his bag into the back of the truck, and then we were heading back to my place. He hadn't said a word the entire time we were at his house, and I found it a little strange. He wasn't quite as tense on the way home, but I noticed he checked his rearview mirror every minute or so. Was he worried that we'd be followed from his place? Or was he just being vigilant in his new role as a bodyguard?

"Thanks for helping me," I told him. Even if I was paying him, he didn't have to agree. He had to have better things to do than babysit me while I figured things out. Assuming I could find a way out of this mess without starting over somewhere else. It didn't seem fair that I was being punished for something Bradley did.

"Maybe I just need the money," he said.

"Or maybe you're a nice guy."

He smiled a little and glanced my way for a brief moment.

At my house, he parked at the curb again. "You can use the driveway."

"The truck leaks oil. It's better if it stays on the street."

"Suit yourself."

I got out and went to open up the house while he got his things. The air conditioning was welcome after being in his hundred-degree house. I tossed my keys onto the table inside the door and waited for Grady to catch up. After I locked the house up behind him, I crooked my finger.

"Follow me and I'll show you to the guest quarters."

"I need a room close to yours if I'm going to protect you. And you'll have to sleep with the door open. Your privacy is going to be invaded while I'm here, but it's the only way to make sure you stay safe."

He followed me upstairs, and I showed him the room next to the master suite. The master had been my parents' room, but it had seemed like a waste of space to not use it after they were gone. I'd only moved in about three months ago, which left my old room for Grady. The white furniture and lavender bedding were a little too feminine for him, but it was only temporary.

"Sorry about the girly colors," I told him. "It used to be my room."

He set his duffle on the floor. "It's fine. Not like I sleep much anyway."

"I'll go order Chinese while you unpack."

Grady shook his head. "I go where you go. The unpacking can wait. If you're going downstairs, I'll go with you."

He reached into his duffle and pulled out a gun, tucking it into the back of his pants. My jaw dropped, and I looked up at him with wide eyes. When the hell had he packed a gun? I hoped it wouldn't be necessary. Bradley was an abusive asshole, but surely he'd turn tail and run the moment he saw Grady.

"Don't worry," Grady said. "It's registered, and I have a concealed carry permit."

My jaw snapped shut. I'd asked if he knew how to use a gun, but I hadn't realized he would actually bring one with him.

"I left my phone in the kitchen earlier." I turned, knowing he would follow, and went downstairs. I flicked on the kitchen light and picked up my phone from the counter. My favorite Chinese place was programmed in, but I pulled out a menu from one of the drawers and gave it to Grady.

He stared at it pretty hard, and I wondered if he just couldn't decide, or if he was trying not to order too much. A guy his size probably could put away a lot of food. I always ordered the same thing, so once I had Grady's order, I could place the call. They usually delivered within a half hour of my call.

"Order anything you want," I told him. "Seriously. If you want one of everything, order it."

He smiled a little. "I'll take a number four and a number eleven with some eggrolls on the side."

I called and placed our order, then went back upstairs. Grady shadowed me, and I wondered if he planned to follow me into the bedroom. I didn't have time for a shower, as much as I would have loved one, so I just grabbed a T-shirt and pulled it over my bikini top. I turned and nearly collided with Grady's massive chest.

"Sorry," he said, stepping out of the way.

"I just wanted to have more clothes on when they delivered the food. I'll need a shower after dinner though."

He nodded. "I'll take a quick one after you go to bed. I'll make sure the house is locked up tight first."

"We can set the alarm. I never really use it, but I know the code. It's the same one my parents used when they were alive. I don't think they shared it with anyone."

At the bottom of the stairs, I veered left and went into the family room. There were four six foot tall bookshelves that were filled with movies. I probably should have let Grady pick, but I was in the mood for something lighthearted, and he seemed more like an action kind of guy. I pulled my favorite movie off the shelf and loaded it into the Blu-ray player.

Before I could sit down, the doorbell chimed. Grady tensed and went to answer it, a hand braced on his weapon. I was grateful for his help, but if he pulled his weapon on the delivery guy I'd never be able to order Chinese again. I ran to the kitchen for my wallet and skidded to a stop at the front door, where Grady was glaring at the teen on the other side. The poor kid looked about ready to piss his pants.

"Miss Sparks, I have your order ready," the kid said.

I thrust the money out to him. "Keep the change and thanks for getting here so fast."

He nodded and practically ran back to his car after he handed over the sack of food. Grady closed and locked the door before turning to face me. He seemed a little disgruntled.

"That kid has the hots for you," he said, taking the sack from me.

I wasn't quite sure what to say to that, so I meekly followed him into the kitchen. I pulled out two plates, and we loaded them up before taking them to the family room to watch the movie. If Grady had a problem with my selection, he didn't say anything. He quietly watched the show while he ate, but I could feel his gaze on me every few minutes. I didn't know if he was making sure I was still here, or if he just liked looking at me. I know I certainly liked looking at him.

Chapter Three

Grady

I had no idea what movie she'd put on, and only half paid attention to it. Instead, I found myself watching Madelyn more than the TV. Even with her split lip and bruised cheek, she was still the most stunning woman I'd ever seen. When she started to doze off, I turned off the TV and lifted her into my arms. She startled awake but just gave me a sleepy smile as I carried her up the stairs. I had no idea how to set the house alarm for the night, so I'd have to be extra vigilant.

In her bedroom, I eased her down onto the bed. There was a blanket folded at the foot, and I pulled it up over her. She sighed in her sleep and snuggled against her pillow. In sleep, she looked even more angelic than she did when she was awake. Some guy was going to be damn lucky to have her in his life one day. I had to assume she was single if she hadn't called on a boyfriend during this ordeal, even though we hadn't discussed her relationship status. Unless that Bradley asshole was her boyfriend, but she'd never called him that.

I left her door open and went into my temporary bedroom. I grabbed my duffle bag and unloaded everything into the empty dresser. Living out of the bag would have been fine, but if she expected me to be here a week, then getting comfortable wasn't going to hurt anything. I removed my shoes and socks, stripped out of my jeans and tee, and stored the gun in the bedside table drawer. After checking on Madelyn one last time, I stretched out on top of the covers so I could roll out of bed with ease if trouble should arise.

I stared at the ceiling, listening for anything that

seemed out of place before closing my eyes. I knew I'd sleep light, but I still didn't relax all the way. Not knowing much about Bradley, I couldn't say whether or not he'd be the type to break in. Any man who put his hands on a woman in anger was slime in my book. But it didn't mean he had the skills to pick a lock. Something about the entire thing bothered me though. Why had he hit her and run? If the man was capable of rape, why wouldn't he have forced her to submit to him? Not that I wished that fate on any woman, but it bothered me.

I hadn't seen any sign of a struggle when I'd gotten to the house, and the police hadn't brought it up. There had been a glass on the counter, yet she hadn't smashed it over his head. So, what had made him run off? I rolled out of bed, grabbed my gun, and prowled through the house, trying to piece everything together in my head. Double checking the locks on the doors and windows, I made my way through each room. A muffled sound caught my attention, and I froze.

"Grady." It was soft, but I heard it.

I bolted up the stairs and down the hall to Madelyn's room, expecting the worst. When I barreled into the room, she was tangled in the blanket and fighting off an imaginary attacker. I eased down onto the mattress and pulled her into my arms, trying to soothe her.

"I'm here, Madelyn. No one is going to get you," I promised.

She quieted and grew still. Slowly, her eyes opened, and she looked up at me. "He was here. He was coming after me again."

"No one's here. It's just you and me."

"Promise?"

"I swear there's no one here but us. You're safe, Madelyn."

"Will you stay with me?"

It would be hell to hold her all night, but I wasn't going to leave her alone if she was that damn scared. I opened the bedside table drawer and almost smiled at the small collection of toys she had tucked in there. Not wanting to mess up any of her vibrators, I stuck the gun on the shelf below the drawer.

Madelyn curled against me, with her head on my chest and her leg thrown across my thigh. I tucked the blanket around her again so she wouldn't catch a chill, and I closed my eyes. Sleeping was impossible with such a delectable woman tucked against me. She made the cutest sounds in her sleep. I couldn't remember the last time I fell asleep holding a woman, couldn't remember having more than a one-night stand in my entire life.

My cock was so damn hard I worried it would break through my boxer briefs. It had been a few weeks since I'd been with a woman, and Madelyn was just too damn tempting. After what she'd been through, the last thing she needed was me lusting after her like some teen who couldn't control himself.

Her soft hand drifted down my abdomen to the waistband of my briefs. My cock jerked in response. Her breath ghosted across my skin as she sighed. Madelyn shifted again, and her knee rose, sliding up my leg to rest just under my balls. If she was intent on killing me, she was doing a damn good job of it.

"I need a shower," she mumbled against me.

The thought of her soaking wet with soap sliding down her long legs didn't help my situation any. I shifted in an effort to get her a little further away from the danger zone. All she did was snuggle closer.

"I'll keep watch out here if you want to get cleaned up," I offered.

Her hand slid a little further down until her palm slid across my very erect cock. "Or you could join me."

My brain short-circuited. That was the only explanation. Surely, she hadn't just suggested that we shower together?

She looked up at me. "I'd feel so much safer with you in there with me."

The mischievous look in her eyes told me that it had nothing to do with safety. Maybe the princess wanted me as much as I wanted her, but I still wondered if it wasn't in response to what had happened to her. There wasn't a textbook way to react to being attacked. Maybe she needed to feel closer to someone?

She tried to shove me off the bed and I stood up, not wanting her to hurt herself. Madelyn slid off the bed and grasped my hand, leading me into the bathroom. The room was about as big as my bedroom at home, with a shower that was definitely big enough for two. She started the water and turned to face me as she shimmied out of her shorts and tossed her tee on the floor. Her swimsuit was just as appealing as it had been out by the pool. When she reached for the strings holding it in place around her neck, my heart gave a kick.

"Are you sure about this, Madelyn?" I asked. "Maybe you should call one of your friends if you need to feel close to someone."

She stopped and stared. "Is that what you think? That I want you to shower with me just because I need to feel close to someone?"

I shrugged.

"Grady, I want you to shower with me because

you're hot as fuck and all I've thought about since I opened my door to you that first day was getting into your pants. I want you, Grady. I need you. But it has nothing to do with what happened today."

My gaze traced the curves of her body. "In that case, princess, strip."

She gave me a saucy smile as she pulled the strings on her top until it fell to the floor at her feet. She shimmied out of the bottoms, and my mouth went dry at the absolute perfection of her. Madelyn came a little closer, reaching for me. Her fingers skimmed along my abdomen and my muscles tensed under her light touch.

I arched a brow as I stared down at her. "Well, what are you waiting for, princess? You going to unwrap that monster cock, or have you changed your mind?"

She peeled my boxer briefs down my legs, and I kicked them away, my cock springing free. I didn't brag -- often -- but I had been more than a little blessed in that department. A good ten inches and too big around for her to hold me with one hand. Her eyes widened. "You want it?" I asked her.

She nodded.

"How much do you want it? You want it bad enough to wrap those pretty lips around it?"

Madelyn whimpered a little as she fell to her knees.

I touched her cheek. "If it's too much at any time, stop. I only want this if it's good for both of us."

"I'll make it so good for you, Grady."

I had no doubt that she would. I bet my little angel could take me straight to heaven. Her tongue lapped at the head of my cock before she fitted those luscious lips around it. Her mouth was hot, wet, and so fucking good I never wanted to leave. She sucked and licked my dick like a damn pro. When she pulled back, her tongue flicked the underside of my cock before she swallowed me down again.

"Baby, I'm gonna blow. If you can't take it, pull away now and wrap those dainty little hands around me."

She sucked harder, and my balls drew up. There was a tingling at the base of my spine, and then I was coming. I watched her through heavy lidded eyes as she swallowed every drop. It seemed my angel was as talented as a porn star, and I couldn't wait to find out what else she could do.

Madelyn climbed to her feet and gave me a hesitant look. "Was that okay?"

"Okay? You blew my mind, princess. What do you say we take that shower before the water gets cold?"

She stepped under the spray, and I followed her, then shut the glass door. The water soaked her honey gold hair and droplets fell from her hard nipples. I reached for her shower gel and lathered my hands before reaching for her. I pulled her out from under the water and massaged the soap into her skin, starting at her throat and working my way down to her cute little toes. Her bare pussy beckoned to me, and I wanted a taste more than anything, but I wasn't going to rush. Who knew when I'd get my hands on a woman like Madelyn ever again?

I lathered her hair and helped her rinse before quickly washing. I turned my back to her in order to rinse my cock and felt her hands coast along my skin. It seemed she wasn't done with me yet, and I smiled a little. I'd had women hunger for me before, but no one like her. She could have any man she wanted with a snap of her fingers, but for some reason she wanted me. I was going to enjoy every minute while it lasted.

There was a little bench on the other end of the shower, and I picked her up and set her down on it. Sinking to my knees at her feet, I spread her legs wide and leaned down to take a taste of paradise. The tang of her arousal coated my tongue as I speared her folds and fucked her tight little pussy.

"Grady!"

I took my time exploring, paying special attention to her hard, little clit, and going back for more of her honey. It wasn't long before she was practically riding my face and begging me for more.

"What do you want?" I asked, my tone harsh from my arousal.

"You. I want you, Grady. Make me yours."

"We're taking this to the bedroom," I told her as I shut off the water.

I tossed her a towel as I quickly dried myself off, and then I threw her over my shoulder and carried her into the bedroom. She hit the bed with a bounce and a giggle. I covered her with my body, kissing her with a hunger I'd never felt before. Her lips were sweet, almost as sweet as the honey I'd sampled in the shower. My cock brushed against her thigh, the tip getting wet from her slick pussy.

"Last chance to back out," I told her.

"Never." She smiled. "I've wanted you for days, Grady."

"Then who am I to deny a princess what she wants?"

I sank into her warmth one inch at a time, giving her body time to adjust. She might not be a virgin, but she was about as tight as one. She hooked her legs over my thighs, opening herself to me. I filled her until my balls brushed against her. I couldn't decide if it was heaven or hell being inside of her. Her satin walls encased me like a glove, and all I could think about was driving into her until I found my release, but I'd be damned if I'd use her like that. *Fuck!* I'd never been inside a woman without a condom before, but for some reason I didn't want any barriers between us.

"You feel amazing," she said, as she gripped my biceps.

"No, princess. You're the one who feels amazing."

And I meant every damn word. She felt incredible as I thrust into her welcoming heat. Our hips slapped together as I pounded that sweet pussy. Her fingers clawed at my arms and shoulders, and her lips were parted on a silent scream. As her body arched into mine, going tense as she threw her head back, I felt her pussy clamp down and try to milk every drop of cum from my balls. I kept thrusting until I had nothing left to give.

Her eyes slowly opened, and she gave me a dreamy smile. "Best. Sex. Ever."

I chuckled and kissed her softly. "I would have to agree."

"Maybe we should rest and then see if it gets better the second time."

My cock grew hard just at the mention of having her again, and I stroked in and out of her a few times. "Why wait when we can go again right now?"

Her eyes widened and her mouth formed an "O" as I tried to take us to paradise for the second time.

Chapter Four
Madelyn

I had aches and twinges in the best of places the next morning. With a smile on my face, I cracked some eggs into a bowl, added a little milk, and beat them until they were nice and frothy. I had a skillet warming on the stove and some bacon in the oven. Grady was doing a perimeter check, or something like that, as I scrambled our eggs. I added a dash of salt and pepper as they cooked. After I pulled the eggs off the stove and added them to our plates, I popped four pieces of bread into the toaster.

By the time Grady came inside, breakfast was ready, and our plates were on the table, accompanied by a glass of juice for each of us. He smiled when he saw the food and held my chair out for me. When I sat, he brushed a kiss against my cheek before claiming his own seat.

"Breakfast looks great," he said.

"I'm not the best cook in the world, but even I can scramble eggs."

"Hey, don't knock it. Scrambling eggs takes talent. I always end up making mine too dry."

"You're probably cooking them at too high a temp. Do you put milk in them?"

He shook his head.

"Try that next time."

"Is there anything you need to do today? Or are we just staying around the house?"

"I should probably go to the grocery store at some point. Did you want to work on the deck some more? Or did you want a day off from it?"

"I'd like to get it finished, but it won't hurt to leave it alone today. I think I have about two more days before it's wrapped up."

"After breakfast, we can head out to the grocery and get it out of the way. If you want to work on the deck later, I can hang out by the pool so you can still keep an eye on me. You're going to be so tired of me by the time this is over."

Grady winked. "No chance of that happening."

I twirled my fork in my hand. "You know, if you really wanted to keep an eye on me all the time, you could just move your things into my bedroom."

He stopped chewing and stared at me.

"Only if you want to."

"Careful there, princess. Inviting me into your bed for more than just a good time could have dire consequences."

"Like what?"

He grinned a little. "Like maybe I won't want to leave."

I didn't have a problem with that. Telling him that probably wasn't the best idea, though. Grady had a look in his eyes like he'd be happy throwing me over his shoulder and carrying me off to the bedroom. Hell. The kitchen counter was closer. After breakfast, I put the dishes in the dishwasher and convinced Grady that it made more sense to take my parents' SUV. I hadn't been able to part with it after their deaths and still used it sometimes. My dad's Corvette had been totaled in the accident that took their lives, and I'd put the insurance money into a savings account.

In the garage, I handed him the keys to the SUV and climbed into the passenger's seat. He reluctantly got behind the wheel and turned the car on.

"Are you sure you want me driving this?" he asked. "It had to have cost a fortune."

"It mostly sits in the garage, Grady. It's fine.

Really."

He handled the car like a pro as he maneuvered the streets of the town. The grocery store parking lot was only half-full since it was still early in the morning. I slid my hand into his as we walked to the front door. The doors opened automatically, and we stepped into the cool interior of the store. I was reluctant to release Grady's hand to grab a shopping cart. He seemed to read my mind and pulled me in front of him, caging me between his arms as he pushed the cart.

His lips pressed against my cheek and butterflies took flight in my stomach. As we tossed things into the cart, I spotted Bradley across the store. I tensed, wanting to turn around and run, but Grady steadily moved us forward.

"I see him," he assured me, which made me wonder if he'd looked Bradley up on the internet at some point. How did he know who Bradley was?

"Can't we just leave and come back later?" I asked.

"No running, princess. Besides, he needs to see that you aren't alone. Might make him think twice about coming back around."

I nodded, but I was still scared as hell.

It didn't take long for Bradley to see us, and I was pleased to see both surprise and a hint of fear on his face when he saw Grady with me. He straightened and headed our way. I didn't have any clue what to say to the man. He'd assaulted me, and because of who his family was, he was going to get away with it. Guys like Bradley made me sick, and unfortunately, they ran rampant in my world. Maybe I should give it all up and move into Grady's bungalow with him.

Whoa. What. The. Fuck. Did I seriously just think

of moving in with Grady after one night? Even I wasn't dumb enough to think that would work. A guy like him would have multiple women ready to do his bidding. I didn't kid myself into thinking I was something special. Just because he'd wanted me didn't mean he wanted happily-ever-after with me. There had been no soft words between us, and I doubted there ever would be.

Bradley stopped his cart next to ours and gave me a smile that didn't reach his eyes. "Good to see you, Madelyn."

"You saw me yesterday."

He cast Grady a nervous glance. "It was all just a misunderstanding, of course."

Grady tensed behind me.

"So, you mistakenly hit me in the face multiple times?" I asked, feeling far braver than normal. I knew even if my mouth got me into trouble that Grady would protect me.

A flash of anger lit up his eyes a moment before he could control it. But it was too late. I'd seen it, and I was certain Grady had too. Bradley might portray himself one way to the world, but he was a vicious asshole underneath the pristine shirts and pressed slacks. You could wrap evil up and put a bow on it, but eventually the darkness would taint the outer wrappings.

"Is he the reason you denied me?" Bradley asked with a jerk of his chin in Grady's direction.

Please don't let Grady be mad at me. "Yes. We've been seeing each other. We're even living together." It wasn't completely a lie. And while I'd known Bradley my entire life, we hadn't been hanging out much since my parents died. I was almost certain he wouldn't know that I'd been living alone all this time, unless someone had mentioned it to him.

Bradley paled a little. "Living together?"

Yeah, asshole, and he's going to kick your ass if you come near me again.

"What can I say? It's hard to deny the princess anything she wants," Grady said, giving my waist a squeeze.

"The truck out front of your house yesterday," Bradley stammered.

"I had an errand to run," Grady said. Then he leaned in close to Bradley. "If you ever so much as darken her doorstep again, if there's even a hint of your preppy stench near the place, I'll make sure your body is never identified and all the pieces aren't found."

Bradley turned damn near green, stammered something unintelligible, and bolted out of the store, leaving his cart behind. I turned and looked up at Grady, wondering if he was angry with me for my deception. Technically, he *had* moved in with me, even if it was only temporary.

He studied me, his gaze unwavering, and I locked my knees. It was an intimidating stare. His eyes gave nothing away, no hint of anger, humor, anything. They were blank, almost as if no one was home. Then that gaze dropped and scanned my body before coming back up. Oh yeah, Grady was in there. And that look said he wanted in *me*.

"Grady, I'm sorry. I shouldn't have…"

He slammed his mouth down on mine, his tongue flicking against mine as he dominated me right in the middle of the produce. I melted under his masterful seduction, my hands clutching at his shirt to remain upright. When he pulled away, there was a hunger blazing in his eyes that made my panties damp and had me whimpering with need.

"You've done it now, princess."

"Wh-what have I done?"

"You just declared that you're mine in front of everyone in this store. And I never let go of anything that's mine."

"Yours?" I squeaked.

He leaned down, his nose brushing against mine. "Mine," he said with a hint of growl to his voice. "And when we get out of this store, I'm very much going to show you just how much you belong to me. When I'm done with you, there will be no doubt in that pretty head of yours that I own your ass."

Oh, shit. Alpha Grady was an even bigger turn-on than tender Grady had been. It seemed I'd unleashed the beast within, and sick bitch that I was, I was looking forward to whatever came next. He had me creaming my panties, ready to grab his hand and take off. Fuck the food. Who needed to eat when there were mind-blowing orgasms to be had?

I sighed a little as he dragged me over to the checkout. It seemed our fun would be put on hold just a little while longer. Even as turned on as he was, it seemed that like a typical guy he was thinking of food.

Chapter Five

Grady

She should have never said she was mine because now that's all I can think about. It's bad enough my cock's been hard since the last time I had her, but now the caveman in me wants to mark her to keep all the other assholes away. Moving into her house was supposed to be temporary, just until preppy boy could be sent packing, but now I'm not so sure I want our time to end. I'm going to see just how far I can push her. See if she bends or breaks. And when I'm done, she'll be ruined for all other men.

I've always been a fuck 'em and leave 'em kind of guy, but there's something about Madelyn that just begs me to break all the rules. I'd never slept with a woman in my arms before, and I had to admit that waking up with her snuggled against me was the best damn morning of my life. At breakfast, I'd wanted to spread her out on the counter and eat her sweet pussy instead of the food she'd fixed, but since she'd gone to so much trouble, I'd behaved myself.

After we loaded the groceries into the back of the SUV, I helped her into the passenger's side and leaned in close, placing my lips against her ear.

"When I close this door, you're going to shimmy out of those shorts and panties."

She gasped and her eyes went wide.

"Nod if you understand, princess."

She slowly nodded and I closed the door, a smirk of satisfaction on my face as I rounded the vehicle and got behind the wheel. I'd gone easy on her so far, not wanting to spook her. But possession was nine tenths of the law, and she'd admitted to being mine. I was more than happy to show her what would happen if I owned her ass. And what an ass it was.

Her cheeks were burning, despite the fact the windows were dark enough no one could see inside. She was so damn cute. Even though she hadn't been a virgin, I had a feeling her experience with men was limited. Hell, I wasn't even certain she'd been with a man before me. Probably one of those boys she hung out with had popped her cherry. Didn't matter. I was going to own every inch of her before the day was over, and she'd be begging me for more.

I backed out of the parking space and headed toward her house, planning to make the most of the trip.

"Spread those legs, princess. Let me see how wet you are."

Her legs parted and the tang of her arousal filled the air. Damn but she smelled good. I reached over and ran my fingers along her slit, gathering her cream, before sucking it off. *Mmm. Tasty.*

I circled her clit, slow lazy circles that had her legs spreading wider.

"Oh, Grady. That feels so good." She moaned and my dick jerked in my pants.

"Do you know what I'm going to do to you today, princess?"

She shook her head, her eyes sliding closed as I dipped my fingers into her core before flicking her clit again.

"I'm going to come in every hole you've got, princess, and you're going to fucking love it. And when I'm done, and you don't think you can take any more, I'm going to have you again. By the time morning comes, you'll be sore and thoroughly fucked."

"Grady." She panted. "So close."

"Does my princess like that? Do you want to

hear about my fat cock pounding into that perfect ass of yours? How you're going to stretch tight around me? I'll be balls deep in that ass, stroking harder, faster, and then I'm going to fill you with my cum."

She cried out, her pussy clenching my fingers as she rode out her orgasm. Who'd have thought my prissy little princess would have liked dirty talk? I chuckled a little at the fun I could have with her before licking my fingers clean.

I was harder than a damn fence post and shifted in my seat to alleviate the pressure. Glancing her way, I saw the contentment on her face. Should I push for more and see just how adventurous she was? She didn't seem like the type to have ever let someone fuck her in a car, and there was only so much I could do while I was driving, but damn if I didn't want more from her.

I freed my cock and sighed in relief. Stroking it a few times, I rubbed the pre-cum down my shaft. It wouldn't take much for me to blow right now. I was an evil bastard for what I was about to ask of her.

"Why don't you take that shirt off and free those tits for me."

She gasped a little and stared at me. "But... the windows..."

"Are tinted. Come on, princess. Get naked for me."

I heard her swallow and then she slowly pulled her shirt over her head and dropped it to the floor before removing her bra. Jesus but those were some gorgeous fucking tits. I'd been mesmerized by them since the first time she'd stepped out of her house in that damn bikini.

"Now, why don't you come over here and give my dick some attention. Up on your knees."

She twisted in her seat so that her ass faced the door as she got onto her knees. Her hands crept across the console and then her hot breath fanned the head of my cock. She moaned a little before wrapping those sweet lips around me. *Fuck!* Her mouth was hot, wet, and fucking incredible. The slurping sounds she made as she sucked my dick just turned me on even more.

My fingers tangled in her hair and I held her still as I thrust upward, shoving my cock to the back of her throat. She swallowed like a damn pro and it was like a dam broke. I started coming, hard and long, fucking her mouth with almost frantic strokes until every last drop of cum was drained from my balls. My eyes nearly crossed and I barely stayed on the road.

"You okay, princess?"

She nodded and smiled at me. "Are we going to play more when we get home?"

"Baby, you're lucky I didn't pull over and fuck you over the hood of the car for everyone to see. You'd better break world records on putting away the cold stuff when we get home, because I plan to have you in the kitchen the moment you're done."

Her eyes dilated and I knew she wanted that as much as I did. Who'd have ever guessed that under that pristine surface was a naughty girl just waiting to break free? No one could have been more perfect for me, and I was going to make damn sure she stayed by my side forever. I'd get her so addicted to my cock she wouldn't be able to go a day without it.

At the house, I pulled into the garage and closed the door before we got out. She might be perfection, but it didn't mean I wanted the entire neighborhood to see her. I carried the bags inside for her, and Madelyn quickly put everything away. She trembled a little when she was finished. "You're really going to take me in the kitchen?" she asked.

"Anyone ever spread you out on the counter to feast on that sweet pussy?"

She shook her head. "I've only been with one guy before and he just wanted to do it the regular way."

My eyebrows arched. "Missionary?"

"Yeah. It… he didn't last very long. It was over almost as soon as it started."

I prowled a little closer. "Are you telling me I was the first man to give you an orgasm?"

"Only you."

"Oh, baby. You shouldn't have told me that. Knowing that I own that piece of you just makes me want more."

She reached out and traced over my muscles. "You can have any part of me you want, Grady. Anytime. Anywhere."

Holy fuck!

With a growl, I lifted her onto the counter and pushed her legs wide apart. I sank to my knees and stared at the perfection of her pussy. She was still wet, her clit still hard. Knowing how much she wanted me was enough to make my cock hard again. The pleasure-seeking bastard was going to have to wait, though. I wanted her screaming my name before I filled that pussy.

I lapped up her cream before spearing her with my tongue. I loved how tight she was and couldn't wait to get inside of her again. I sucked her clit into my mouth and lashed it with my tongue. Madelyn tensed and cried out as her hips bucked. I drew on the nub long and hard before tongue fucking her again. I sucked, licked, teased. She was writhing on the counter and chanting my name when I finally made her come with a scream that damn near rattled the windows.

She lay panting and spent as I rose to my feet, my jeans still pushed down around my hips. I stripped off my shirt and pulled her ass closer to the edge of the counter. The head of my cock bumped her clit once. Twice. Three times before I slid inside of her fast, hard, and deep. She cried out and her pussy clenched down on me.

"What does my princess want?"

"I want you to fuck me."

I drew out slowly and thrust back in, slowly feeding her all ten inches of my cock. "Like that?"

"No." She whimpered. "Faster. Harder."

I gripped her hips and gave her a pounding she wouldn't soon forget. She screamed out my name twice more before I came inside of her. I had some primal need to mark her with my cum and stayed buried in her warmth to make sure none of it escaped. We hadn't discussed birth control and fuck me if I cared right then. The thought of her swollen with my child almost made me come again.

I wanted that. I wanted her.

I pulled out, kicked off my jeans, and lifted her into my arms, carrying her upstairs. When we got to the bedroom, I laid her out on the bed and admired her sexy curves. My cum dripped down her thighs, but she didn't make a move to wipe it away. I climbed onto the bed with her.

I'd barely pulled her into my arms before she was already asleep. It seemed multiple orgasms had worn her out. I'd let her rest a while, and then I'd take her again. I hadn't lied. She was going to be sore tomorrow, every step reminding her that she was mine.

Chapter Six

Madelyn

Grady had completely rocked my world the last few days. I hadn't heard another peep out of Bradley, and I wondered if he was too damn scared to face off against Grady. Which meant the moment his truck wasn't parked in front of my house anymore, Bradley would come around again. I didn't know what the hell I was going to do. I wanted Grady to stay, and not just because of Bradley. I was falling for him -- hard. I just wasn't sure if he felt the same way about me.

I watched across the pool as he finished off the deck. It looked amazing, and I had to admit he was very talented with his hands -- in more ways than one. He stood and stretched, and I drooled a little. No one was sexier than Grady. And damn if he didn't know it. He didn't act conceited or overly arrogant though, not like you'd expect of someone who looked like a Greek god. The way he touched me, it was almost like he was afraid I'd disappear sometimes. Other times, he took me with a force that left me breathless and wanting more.

He put his tools away, checked on me, then disappeared out the back gate. I'd told him that he could store his tools in the garage, but he didn't want to make a mess. Hell, as far as I was concerned, he could make a work space out of the unused space out there. If he stayed, if I could convince him I wanted forever, then I'd surprise him with a work bench either in the garage or I'd have a new building added to the property just for him. There was room near the garage in the space designated for a boat or RV, neither of which I owned.

I heard something in the house shatter and I took

off, worrying that Grady might have gone through the front door and hurt himself. I went skidding to a stop just inside the kitchen, looking at the broken shards on the floor, but there was no sign of Grady. Thankfully, there wasn't a drop of blood either.

"Grady!" I called out, tiptoeing around the mess to look for him.

Another crash sent me running to the family room, where a bookcase of movies had been knocked over. What the hell? I tensed when I felt a presence behind me, and it didn't feel like Grady. I spun and my eyes widened when I saw Bradley. He held a syringe of something in his hand and advanced on me.

"What do you want?" I demanded, in a tone that wasn't as steady as I would have liked. But damn if I wasn't scared shitless. Where was Grady? No way he'd have let Bradley slip past him.

"We're going to have a little time to ourselves. No one will find that stupid boyfriend of yours anytime soon. I gave him a shot of this and dragged his ass into the bushes." Bradley smirked. "Bet you didn't think I was that strong."

"You're a spineless coward is what you are. You're not man enough to take Grady face to face. You know he'd have pummeled your ass."

Something dark crossed his face before he grabbed my arm and hauled me closer. There was a prick as the needle went in and I cried out as he plunged the liquid into my body. Everything spun and my legs gave out. I opened my mouth, but nothing came out, and I couldn't move my arms or anything else. It was horrible! I was awake and knew everything that was happening, but I was unable to fight back. What had the bastard given me?

He lifted me into his arms and carried me

upstairs. At least he wasn't taking me to some unknown place, where Grady would have a hard time finding me. Tears streaked my cheeks as he carried me into what had been my old bedroom. I guessed he didn't know that I'd moved into my parents' room. He didn't even bother closing the door as he gave me a sinister smile and started stripping out of his clothes.

After being with Grady, Bradley seemed small and weak, even if I was at his mercy. His muscles were almost non-existent and his dick was just damn pathetic. If I'd been able to speak, I'd have told him as much. He started to remove my bikini, but something stopped him. He froze, tilting his head as he listened. Then the sinister smile was back and he pulled off my swimsuit top. He was reaching for my bottoms when Grady staggered into the doorway, a murderous look on his face.

He leaned against the doorframe and shook his head, letting me know that I wasn't to tell Bradley about his presence. My heart raced as Bradley fumbled with the strings on the bottoms of my swimsuit. Grady seemed to find his balance and he prowled into the room, as silent and graceful as a panther. He pressed the end of his gun to Bradley's temple and my attacker froze, his eyes wide with fright.

"It's going to take more than that to knock me out, you stupid fucker."

A very feminine whimper escaped Bradley and the stench of urine filled the room. Had he seriously just pissed his pants? I wanted to laugh, but whatever he'd given me still had my body unresponsive.

"You kill me, and you'll go to jail," Bradley said. "My father…"

"I don't give a shit about your father. What you don't know is that I put surveillance cameras in every room in this damn house a few days ago. Which means I have you on camera hauling Madelyn up here, and I think it's going to be obvious what you planned. There are also cameras outside, which recorded you trying to knock my ass out."

Bradley paled. "I'll give you whatever you want. Money. Cars. A new house? It's yours. Just name your price."

"Is that how you got out of it all those other times? You bought their silence?" Grady demanded. "Guess what, fucker. I can't be bought."

Grady threw a blanket over me. I opened my mouth to thank him, but not much came out.

"It's okay, princess. The cops are on the way and once this asshat is taken care of, we'll get you checked out." There was a hardness in Grady's eyes as he stared at Bradley. "And this time, the asshole isn't going to get away with attacking you."

Relief flooded me. Not only that Grady had arrived in time, but that Bradley would have to pay for his crimes this time. He'd gotten away with too much in his life. I had no doubt his family would try to keep things as quiet as possible so their precious name wasn't tarnished, but I hoped Bradley's face was plastered over all the main news stations so everyone would know what he really was.

When the cops arrived, they requested an ambulance since I still hadn't gotten complete control of my body and voice, even though I could now move my fingers and toes. Grady handed over the tapes proving that Bradley had intended both of us harm and had broken into the house. I had no idea if they were originals or copies. The officers thought that the District Attorney would be very appreciative of the footage and said someone would be in touch.

The ambulance arrived and the EMTs checked me over. Grady wouldn't let them near me until he'd cleared the room and put my top back on and made sure my bottoms were secure. Even then, he hovered, watching every move they made. If they touched me in a way he deemed inappropriate, he growled at them and gave them a look that nearly had them scurrying out of the room.

By the time they convinced him I needed a hospital, my voice was slowly coming back. I still couldn't move much though. The doctor in the ER said I needed to stay overnight for observation, which pissed Grady off.

"Why are you so mad?" I asked.

"I don't like seeing you hooked up to all these machines. I could have taken care of you at home."

I smiled, liking that he called it home. Now that Bradley was gone, we'd have to discuss our relationship. For now, I was just going to enjoy the fact he was staying close and watching over me. He stretched out in the recliner by the bed and glared at anyone who came near me. It was sweet. No one had ever watched over me like Grady did. I just hoped he was up for doing it long-term.

"Thank you for coming after me," I told him.

"It was my job, right?" His jaw tensed.

"Is that all it was?" I asked softly. Had the last few days not meant as much to him?

"I'm a guy from the wrong side of the tracks and you're practically royalty."

"What's that supposed to mean?"

"You think I didn't do some research on you the last several days? I know your mother is related to the president. You'd have found a way to hand Bradley his ass without my help. All you had to do was make a phone call."

I winced. "I wasn't trying to keep the connection from you. No one knows about it. Mom worried that I would be in danger if anyone ever found out, so she made me swear to not tell."

"Then why did you call me that night? Why not have it taken care of? I would think an attack would be a good reason to make that connection known."

"Because you make me feel safe. You make me feel more than that. I've wanted you since the moment I opened my door that day. I wasn't lying about that. I guess I just wanted some alone time with you. Was that so wrong?"

"You put yourself in jeopardy just to have some quality time with me?" he asked.

"Maybe." I bit my lip.

"And you didn't think of just asking me out on a date?"

"Would you have accepted?"

He hesitated.

"That's what I thought." I frowned. "So, was our time together just because of our circumstances? Would you have walked away after the deck was finished and never looked back?"

His stared at me, but didn't answer. That was answer enough for me. Here I'd been falling in love, and I'd just been convenient for him. I should have known. What would a guy like Grady want with someone like me? I had very little experience with men, and I'd thought surely he felt the same about me. Maybe sex was always that hot with him, no matter who he was with.

I fought back tears as I looked at him for what I knew would be the last time. My throat ached from the need to cry and I managed to get myself under control long enough to tell him to go.

"You've done your job," I told him. "I'll have your check couriered to your house after they release me from the hospital."

"So, that's it?" he asked.

"You obviously don't want to be here with me, Grady. I'm not going to force you to do something you don't want to do."

He nodded and stood. "I'll leave your key on the counter after I collect my things."

As he walked out the door, I allowed myself to cry. Sobs racked my body as I cried for everything I'd ever wanted, and knew I'd never have. Because the only man I'd ever love was Grady, and he thought I was some spoiled princess who was too far above him. And there wasn't a damn thing I knew to do to fix it.

By the time they released me the next morning, my stomach was aching. I didn't want to go home to an empty house. I called a friend to take me home, who asked more questions than I wanted to answer. She dropped me in the driveway and I dug through the purse Grady had brought to the hospital to find my keys. When I let myself in, I was surprised the living room was put back in order. I made my way back to the kitchen and found all of the glass cleaned up too.

Had Grady taken care of it? And if so, what did it mean? Would someone who didn't care take the time to do that?

Upstairs, I stopped at my old room. The sheets were folded and stacked on the bare mattress, and I wondered if Grady had washed them to remove the taint of what had happened. In my bedroom, I face planted on the bed and breathed in his scent on the sheets. Tears sprang to my eyes and I worried that I would miss him the rest of my life. Wanting to keep my promise of payment, I went back downstairs and wrote him a check in the amount we'd agreed upon for him guarding me in addition to the amount for the deck. Then I called a courier service and had it delivered to him.

It felt so final… and my heart broke further.

Chapter Seven

Grady

Two weeks had passed since I'd left the hospital, and walked away from the best thing that ever happened to me. There was no way it would have lasted, or at least that's what I told myself often. The look in her eyes as I'd shut her out had nearly destroyed me. She was safe now, though, in her big house with all her rich friends. She didn't need me anymore. Her check had arrived the next day without so much as a note. It told me all I needed to know. She was moving on and that was what I needed to do. Just as soon as I figured out how.

My friends had talked me into hanging out at the local bar for drinks, which had quickly turned into them trying to get me laid. Something I wasn't interested in. I could still remember Madelyn's scent when I closed my eyes at night. I'd cashed her check, not because I wanted to but because I was desperate for food and air conditioning. I'd replaced all the units in my house and had stocked the fridge with beer and the pantry with quick meals to make. The beer interested me more than the food.

"What the hell is wrong with you?" my buddy Rob groused. "Since when do you turn down easy pussy?"

Since Madelyn. Not that I was going to tell him that.

My other friend, Sam, just shook his head. "Can't you tell the guy is brokenhearted? Whatever had him MIA a few weeks back did a number on him. I'm guessing it was a woman."

"That right?" Rob asked as he took a swig of his beer. "You hung up on some woman?"

I shrugged and stared at my beer. Madelyn wasn't just some woman, but neither of these guys would understand. We'd grown up together, and I couldn't see either of them being sympathetic that I fell for a girl from the other side of the tracks. We'd always steered clear of those type of women, and for good reason. They might want to walk on the wild side every now and then, but at the end of the day they married doctors and lawyers. Not broke handymen.

"Whatever is in your head, throw it out," Sam said. "I can tell you really like this woman. So what the hell are you doing sitting here with us?"

"She's better off without me."

Sam shook his head. "Bullshit. You're a great guy, Grady. Did you tell her that you'd won the Medal of Honor when you were a Marine? Chicks dig that shit."

"What does it matter?" I asked. "I'm not a Marine anymore. I'm just the handyman who lives on the questionable side of town in a house that's falling apart. What the hell could I offer her?"

"Your heart?" Sam asked softly. "Because I'm pretty sure you already gave it to her. Look, we all fall for that perfect girl, the one we can never have. But maybe this time she's not as unattainable as you think. Instead of sitting here missing her, why don't you haul your ass out to your truck and go talk to her?"

Rob snorted. "Nothing good will come of it."

"Shut up, asshole," Sam said. "Just because Wendy won't give you the time of day doesn't mean you need to tell Grady his love is doomed."

Rob shot him the bird.

"You really think she'd even speak to me after the way I left?" I asked.

"You won't know unless you try," Sam said.

I downed my beer and stood, maybe a little unsteady. Should I drive? I thought about Madelyn and the urge to see her grew until I couldn't deny myself just a glimpse. I pulled my keys from my pocket and went out to the parking lot to climb into my truck. I drove slow on the way to Madelyn's, the lines on the road blurring a little. When I pulled up out front of her house, the driveway was empty and the living room lights were on.

Stumbling out of my truck, I slammed the door and walked up to the house. I rang the bell and weaved on my feet while I waited for her to appear. I just need one look at my regal princess, just one look to take away the loneliness I'd been feeling.

"Madelyn!" I yelled out.

The volume on the TV went up higher and I frowned. She had to know it was me. Was she really done with me? Had I screwed up so bad that she didn't even want to see me anymore? I rang the bell and beat my fist against the door, but still she didn't answer.

I heard a car pull up and I turned around, my eyes widening in surprise at the officer that stepped out of the black and white vehicle.

"Son, is there a problem?" the older officer asked.

"She won't talk to me," I mumbled. "Just want to see her."

"I suggest you sober up before you talk to her." He looked from me to the truck and back again. "You drive here in that condition?"

I didn't confirm or deny.

The officer sighed. "All right. I say we let you sleep it off in the drunk tank tonight. You can come talk to your girl tomorrow, when you're not so drunk you can't stand up straight."

When he led me by the arm to his waiting car, I

didn't protest. I glanced back longingly at the house and saw the blinds move, knowing that she saw me. The officer shoved me into the backseat and slammed the door before climbing behind the wheel and pulling away. I'd spent a night or two in the drunk tank before, but never because of a woman.

The precinct wasn't far and we arrived faster than I would have liked.

There were three other guys in the cell when he shoved me inside. Two were snoring loudly and the other was singing "Oklahoma" off-key. I plopped my ass down and slammed my head back against the cinder block wall. Of all the ways I'd thought I'd spend my night, in jail had never crossed my mind. I'd hoped to be reunited with Madelyn, in her bed, all night long. Instead, she'd called the cops on me. Guess that told me all I needed to know. She didn't want a damn thing to do with me.

When morning came, and my head felt like someone was hammering at my skull, my buddy Sam picked me up and took me back to my truck. I tried not to look at her house as I got in and drove home. She'd made her choice. If she didn't want anything to do with me, then I wouldn't taint her house with my presence. It sucked ass, but I wasn't going to force myself on her. I loved her, dammit. Loved her more than I'd ever loved anyone, and she didn't love me back. I knew I was never going to get over Madelyn. She was a once in a lifetime kind of woman, and I'd fucked up because I'd turned chicken shit at the hospital. Now I had to live with it.

Sam pulled up behind me at my house. "You need some company?"

"I'll be fine."

"Does that mean you'll be drowning your

sorrows? Because that isn't going to get you some steady work. She may have paid you for the job at her place, but that doesn't mean the money will last forever. You need to work, Grady. It might take your mind off things."

I nodded. "I have some calls to return. Maybe I'll do that."

"I'm just a call away if you decide you want company." Sam got back in his truck and pulled away.

I let myself into the house and pulled out my cell phone. Three people had called in the last few days wanting quotes for anything from a fence to adding on a nursery to their master suite. I didn't know if they were referrals from Madelyn or not. I hadn't asked, and I didn't know that I wanted to. I lined up some quotes for the next two days and tried to keep busy, tinkering around the house when I wasn't working. The next few days passed quickly, but the ache in my chest didn't go away.

She'd kept her promise. Two of the quotes had come from people Madelyn knew. She'd told them what a great job I'd done on her deck and now they wanted me to help with their projects. I should have been thrilled because they were expensive jobs that would bring in a good amount of cash. But all I could think about was Madelyn, and how much I missed her.

I spent two weeks adding a room onto the master suite for one of her married friends, and then moved on the fence project that was going to take another week. I'd been on the job five days and was nearly finished when a shadow fell across me. I looked up the long tan legs to the barely-there bikini and finally settled on her face. Her lips were pursed and her hands were on her hips.

"I've done everything I can think of to get your

attention," she said.

"Did you need something?" I asked, dropping my hammer into the toolbox and standing.

"I've practically been throwing myself at you."

Oh. I wasn't certain how to respond to that. It wasn't that she wasn't attractive, but she wasn't Madelyn. I scratched the back of my neck and stared down at her, not knowing what to say.

"You love her, don't you?" she asked softly. "She said you didn't want her, but that's not true."

"Madelyn doesn't want me."

"Madelyn is scared shitless right now," she said. "And just so you know, she's not the one who had you arrested. Her neighbor called the cops."

I shrugged. She still hadn't come out to see me. What was the difference?

"I think you need to see her," the woman said.

What was her name? Brittany? Bethany? Something with a B in it.

"She doesn't want to see me." I picked up my tools. "I'll come by in the morning. I might be able to finish tomorrow afternoon."

"She misses you. I know you don't believe me, but she does. I was supposed to meet her tonight for dinner at her place. She said she'd leave the front door unlocked around seven o'clock."

"Why are you telling me this?" I asked.

"Because I think that gives you enough time to go home and shower and surprise her."

I snorted. "And get arrested for breaking in?"

"It's not breaking in if the door is unlocked. Just go see her. Believe me, you need to."

With that cryptic message, I hauled ass out to my truck and drove home. The last thing I needed to do was go to Madelyn's and have her call the cops.

Despite what her friend said, I seriously doubted she wanted to see me.

But what if she does?

Indecision weighed heavy on me. After I showered at home, I stared at my wallet and keys and finally decided that I was going to confront Madelyn and hear it straight from her lips whether or not she wanted me to leave her alone.

I could only hope she'd missed me as much as I'd missed her.

* * *

Madelyn

Bridget was due any minute and I was tossing the salad when I heard the front door open. My stomach gurgled and I wasn't sure if it was from hunger or if I was about to throw up again. Whoever called it morning sickness was an asshole, because it was all damn day sickness. When Grady had left, he'd left a little something behind. My eyes misted as I thought about him. I'd kicked myself for not opening the door the night he'd shown up, even if he had sounded drunk off his ass. I knew he'd never hurt me.

The front door open and shut. "I'm in the kitchen," I called out.

The clunking steps that drew nearer didn't sound like Bridget. Unease skittered down my spine, and I nearly cried with relief when Grady stepped into the room. He looked so damn good. My knees went a little weak just looking at him and my heart raced in my chest.

"Grady," I said in almost a whisper.

"Your friend suggested I come in her place," he said as he came closer. "But if you want me to leave, I'll turn around and head out right now."

I shook my head. "Stay."

"I'm sorry for showing up drunk. I just wanted to see you."

"I'm sorry I didn't open the door. I was just so hurt from you leaving me the way you did, but after you left I'd wished I'd let you in. I didn't mean for the neighbors to call the cops on you."

"They were trying to protect you."

"I don't need protecting from you."

He smiled a little.

"I made lasagna and a spinach salad. Are you hungry?"

"Starving."

I picked up the salad bowl and carried it over to the kitchen table, where the lasagna was already waiting, along with two place settings and two glasses of sweet tea. He claimed the seat he'd used during the days he'd spent with me and I took the other as butterflies erupted in my stomach. Grady was here. He was really here. I needed to tell him that he was going to be a daddy, but I thought I should at least wait until after dinner. The man needed to eat and he could very well bolt out the door when I said something.

I fixed our plates and watched as he took a bite, his eyes closing and a look of bliss on his face.

"You're a damn good cook, princess. Why didn't you make this while I was staying here?"

"I wanted to spend more time with you and not in the kitchen cooking."

He nodded.

"Grady, I've missed you."

"Missed you too, princess. So damn much."

He reached over and took my hand. I trembled just from that slight touch and nearly cried with how much I'd missed him. *Stupid pregnancy hormones.*

We ate and took turns staring at one another. It felt so right having Grady with me again. I hoped that maybe this time he wouldn't run off and leave me. Just because he'd surprised me tonight didn't mean he was here for the long haul. And now I had more than just me to worry about. I needed to do whatever was right for my baby. Was that why Bridget had set this up? Had she told him about me being pregnant? My stomach knotted and a moment later I bolted out of my chair and ran for the downstairs bathroom, barely making it before I lost what little I'd eaten.

"Madelyn?" Grady stopped in the bathroom doorway and then he was holding my hair and rubbing my back. "Jesus. Are you okay? Have you been sick?"

"Not sick," I croaked before throwing up again.

When I was finished, he helped me rinse my mouth and sat on the floor, pulling me into his arms. He pressed a kiss to the top of my head and just cuddled me.

"Madelyn, are you pregnant?" he asked, and I felt like the bottom fell out. Moment of truth.

"Yes."

He nibbled my near. "And it's mine?"

I nodded.

"Were you going to tell me?" he asked.

"I didn't know how. You didn't want me, so why would you want a baby?"

He cursed. "I'm sorry, princess. I never should have made you feel like you weren't wanted. I've missed you every damn day I've been gone. And I want this baby." His hand cupped my stomach. "I want both of you."

"You're not just saying that?" I asked.

"No, princess. I'm not just saying that. Don't you

know?"

"Know what?"

"How much I love you."

My eyes teared as I clung to him. "I love you too, Grady. So much. I nearly died when you walked out of my hospital room. I thought I'd never see you again."

I stood and reached for the toothbrush and toothpaste I'd started leaving down here for emergencies. I brushed my teeth and then led him back to the kitchen, but before we could reach the table, he stopped. Looking up at him, I marveled at how handsome he was, and felt a thrill that he was mine.

"We're going to finish dinner, and then you're going to pick a movie while your food settles. But when we go to bed tonight, I'm going to prove to you all night long how much I love you and how damn sorry I am." He pressed a kiss to my lips before swatting me on the ass.

"You took all your things home."

"I packed an overnight bag just in case you were in a forgiving mood." He grinned.

"You're going to need more than an overnight bag." I licked my lips. "I know you have your own place, but I want you to live here with me, Grady. The house has been so damn lonely without you in it."

"I can't think of anything I'd like more, princess."

We finished our dinner, then cuddled on the couch and watched a movie together. When it was over, Grady lifted me into his arms and carried me upstairs to our bedroom, where he made good on his promise, and loved me all night long.

Who'd have ever guessed that hiring a hunky handyman would have turned my world completely upside down, but in the best of ways?

Harley Wylde

Harley Wylde is the International Bestselling Author of the Dixie Reapers MC, Devil's Boneyard MC, and Hades Abyss MC series. When Harley's writing, her motto is the hotter the better -- off the charts sex, commanding men, and the women who can't deny them. If you want men who talk dirty, are sexy as hell, and take what they want, then you've come to the right place. She doesn't shy away from the dangers and nastiness in the world, bringing those realities to the pages of her books, but always gives her characters a happily-ever-after and makes sure the bad guys get what they deserve.

The times Harley isn't writing, she's thinking up naughty things to do to her husband, drinking copious amounts of Starbucks, and reading. She loves to read and devours a book a day, sometimes more. She's also fond of TV shows and movies from the 1980's, as well as paranormal shows from the 1990's to today, even though she'd much rather be reading or writing. You can find out more about Harley or enter her monthly giveaway on her website. Be sure to join her newsletter while you're there to learn more about discounts, signing events, and other goodies!

More books by Harley Wylde at changelingpress.com/harley-wylde-a-196

Changeling Press E-Books

More Sci-Fi, Fantasy, Paranormal, and BDSM adventures available in e-book format for immediate download at ChangelingPress.com -- Werewolves, Vampires, Dragons, Shapeshifters and more -- Erotic Tales from the edge of your imagination.

What are E-Books?

E-books, or electronic books, are books designed to be read in digital format -- on your desktop or laptop computer, notebook, tablet, Smart Phone, or any electronic e-book reader.

Where can I get Changeling Press E-Books?

Changeling Press e-books are available at ChangelingPress.com, Amazon, Apple Books, Barnes & Noble, and Kobo/Walmart.

Changeling Press, LLC

ChangelingPress.com

Printed in Great Britain
by Amazon

29863175R00129